# ALL GODS MUST BE LEASHED

"Have you been here very long?" Marianne asked.

"Off and on," said the Black Dog. "When we had time."

"I thought maybe . . . maybe you'd gone back to—to wherever *Marianne* got you from."

"She got us from our own loci," the Foo Dog said. "Every locus in the universe has one of us attendant to it. We give material space its reality by giving time its duration. Each moment is dependent upon us. Hence, momentary gods."

"But if you're not in your proper—locus, then what happens to the universe?" she asked.

"We're there," said the Foo Dog. "And here. Being in two places at once is very common for a momentary god . . ."

*Praise for MARIANNE, THE MAGUS, AND THE MANTICORE*

"A most enjoyable novel . . . very elegantly done . . . Tepper's quirky prose is very well suited to Marianne's eccentricities, and serves to make the character all the more plausible."
—*Locus*

"If you like suspenseful fantasy, this is the one for you!"
—*Compuserve*

"Danger   mys-terious!"

—*ates*

# SHERI S. TEPPER

# MARIANNE, THE MADAME, AND THE MOMENTARY GODS

ACE BOOKS, NEW YORK

This book is an Ace original edition,
and has never been previously published.

MARIANNE, THE MADAME, AND THE MOMENTARY GODS

An Ace Book/published by arrangement with
the author

PRINTING HISTORY
Ace edition/December 1988

ISBN: 0-441-51962-8

Ace Books are published by The Berkley Publishing Group,
200 Madison Avenue, New York, New York 10016.
The name ''ACE'' and the ''A'' logo are trademarks belonging to Charter
Communications, Inc.

PRINTED IN THE UNITED STATES OF AMERICA

10  9  8  7  6  5  4  3  2  1

# CHAPTER 1

THERE WERE NO words in her mind at all. None of the tools of thinking were there, not yet. Nonetheless, she saw faces peering down at her, saw smiles on lips, heard chortling words and knew them. They were people. The words of recognition came swimming through her mind like familiar fish. Mama. Papa. Great-aunt Dagma.

She was three days old.

The room was as familiar as the people. Light came from the right, moving in a recognized way as the wind stirred the curtains at the tall window. She already knew the tree outside that window, already knew the lawn beneath that tree. On her fourth birthday there would be a pony tethered there for her birthday gift.

She knew the house, every closet and attic of it. There were no rooms in it that she was not already aware of, knowing the boundaries and smell and feel of them, tight wall or loose, small window or large, the wonderful magic of familiar-familial spaces. There was porch space, half open, half shut in, where tree shadows made walls and the spaces between branches made windows for the wind to reveal and the sun to dart through. There was cavernous attic space, smelling of dust

1

and dead moth bodies, stacked with sealed boxes as mysterious as old people, full of experiences she had not had yet, was not certain she wanted, yet anticipated with a kind of wondering inevitability. There were long, carpeted halls with windows at the ends and dark in the middle, the twining vines and exotic fruits on the rugs making a safe path down the center from light to light. There were bedrooms, each breathing of a special inhabitant with scent and aura peculiar to that one. There was a deep, stone-floored kitchen that begged for a witch's cauldron and a dragon on the hearth.

She already knew them all.

She was not aware that this knowledge was in any respect abnormal or unusual. This was the way of her world. The place was known. *Her* place was known.

Her people, too, were known. Cloud-haired Mama with her soft skin and smiling mouth; bearded Papa with his hard laugh and huge, swallowing hugs; Great-aunt Dagma with her jet-black brows and lashes under hair as white as snow, with eyes that twinkled sometimes and bit sometimes like sharp little puppy teeth. Marianne could see into all of them as though they were glass.

Except for half-brother Harvey. He, too, stood at the cribside, making admiring noises in his suddenly bass, suddenly treble thirteen-year-old voice, but when she looked at him she could not see beyond the surface of his eyes. He was like the pool in the garden when it got muddied after rain, cloudy, hiding everything. One knew there were fish in there, but one could not see them. One could only guess at their cold trajectories, their chilly purposes, and the guessing made one shiver with apprehension. So with Harvey. She did not know him, and awareness of this blighted an otherwise perfect understanding of everything around her. Not that she thought of it in this way. If she acknowledged it at all, it was simply to identify Harvey as different and scary. He, unlike anything else in her environment, was capable of being and doing the utterly unexpected.

When she was three, they took her to the city.

The motion of the car put her to sleep, and when she awoke, she saw through the window of the car an endless procession of stranger houses. Each house was tight against the next, all of them staring out at the street in a glare of hard, blue light, watching her. She began to scream.

Mama picked her up and cuddled her, asking her what it was that hurt and whether it was teeth or tummy. It was neither. It was the sight of that endless row of stranger houses that had frightened her half out of her infant wits. They were the first closed places she had ever seen, the first unfamiliar sights or sounds in her life, and they came as a hideous surprise.

If Papa had not had to take a detour, they would have gone through a park. Somehow, she remembered a park. The picture of the park superimposed itself on the row of houses and she fell asleep again. There should have been a park.

Thereafter, from time to time, she experienced similar superimpositions, as though her life were a palimpsest on which one experience was written over another in confusing detail so it was difficult to know which was real and which was something else. Not less real, she thought as she began to be old enough to think about things. Simply less relevant to the other things that were going on.

Her second encounter with a closed, unfamiliar place came a year or so later, when she was old enough to go for long walks. Her hand held tightly in Nanny's hand, she strolled down the driveway and out onto the country road. She remembered turning left, but they actually turned right to walk down the road toward the river, passing on the way a tall, gray stone house set well back from the road with windows that stared at her from half-lowered lids. Its door pursed its sill and scowled. As in that time she had visited the city, she wept. She couldn't tell Nanny what was wrong, she hadn't the words for it, and everyone assumed some childhood indisposition when it wasn't that at all. It was simply that she did not know the gray house.

Every morning she could remember, Marianne had awakened knowing the people and places and events that day would bring. Each event was ready for her in her recollection, even before she experienced it, as well as the consequences of that event, sometimes far in the future. If she helped the gardener plant bulbs, the ultimate flowers were already there in her mind, though she would not actually see the blooms until spring. As she was lifted onto her pony for the first time, she already remembered learning to ride it. The horse she would love so much would come later, and the memory of that future horse was evoked by the present pony even as she struggled to master the muscles needed to stay on. Her body experienced it for the first time, but her mind—it already *knew*. It needed only a clue to come to mind. Bulb evoked flower. Pony evoked horse. All her teachers were amazed. "She seems to soak it up like a little sponge," her riding teacher said, laughing a little uncomfortably. It seemed unfair to the other children that this one should take it all in so easily.

She assumed, for a time, at least, that everyone lived as she did, knowing what would come before it happened, knowing the places they lived in as soon as they were born. She assumed everyone had occasional visions of some alternate reality, sometimes dull, sometimes bright, sometimes frightening and bizarre. She did not know that she was unique, that no one else in the world lived as she did. She was unwilling to accept that there might be people and places that remained strangers. Instead she chose to believe that the knowledge would come later. She would get to know them someday. Someday there would be no more unfamiliar streets, no more closed doors, no more shut windows. Someday, when she was grown-up, everything would be understood. The gray house, with all its spaces, its roofs and porches, its closets and attics would come to her, part of growing up. She would be able to greet it as she walked on the street. "Hello old green-shingly-with-the-cupola. Still have that mouse family in the attic?" Someday, she told herself comfortingly, intercepting a hard, opaque stare from her half brother, she might know Harvey, too. It would come. She would use the huge, old gray stone house as a yardstick to determine whether the time had come or not.

The season came when she started to school, and for the first time she began to suspect she might be different from other children. Why should she enter the school on the first day knowing everything about it, while other children cowered and cried as though it were new and strange? Other children did not know where their classrooms were. Why did she? They did not know where the bathrooms were or where the drinking fountain had made a weirdly shaped yellow stain on the wall, like an upside-down giraffe. To Marianne it was all as familiar as though studied in advance. Why should she know her teacher's name before they met when other children didn't know? She had to accept the fact that they did not know, and in doing so she learned of her own strangeness. She did not want it to show, so she learned to counterfeit surprise and mimic apprehension. Still, she could never do so without feeling that somehow she was lying.

She walked to school each day, often going out of her way to pass the great gray house. Each day she peeked at it, quick, birdlike glances, waiting for the day when it would open like a flower with all its high stairs and dormer windows, waiting for the first glimmer of recognition. That year, the year she was six, went by and the house did not open. Nor when she was seven, or eight.

Still, she believed it would happen. She believed it for a long time, until one day she talked to Great-aunt Dagma, who was very old and thus of an age to have opened all the places of the world, and found that Great-aunt Dagma didn't know the gray house at all.

"Why, child, I haven't any idea," she said. "I've never been in it. It's occupied by some people called Carlson, I believe, but as to whether it has an attic or not? I just don't know."

So the house really was a stranger house. So were the houses in the city. Strangers. Not understood. Marianne sat there, in a state of profound shock, unable to speak for a long time. Great-aunt Dagma was a sympathetic listener who did not make fun, however, and at last Marianne was able to confess that the house was very strange to her. "Not like home, Great-aunt," she confided. "It seems like—oh, like somebody who doesn't talk our language at all. Some people are like that, too. Harvey's like that."

Great-aunt, with a strangely intent look, agreed that this described Harvey very well. "He does always seem to be saying one thing with his mouth and something else with his eyes, doesn't he, Marianne. Ah, but then, he's always been a tight, closed boy, like a treasure box with the key hidden away somewhere. His mother was like that, herself, and his aunt is a perfect example. Lubovoskans, you know. It's a strange, shaman-ridden, paranoid country, Lubovosk—unlike sunny Alphenlicht from which our family comes—so it's no wonder the people show that characteristic. Harvey is a hard boy to get to know. Don't let it worry you, child. It isn't your fault.''

Marianne had not thought it was her fault. Still, the implication was inescapable, and she was neither so stubborn nor so unintelligent as to miss it. Merely growing up would not open the gray house or her half brother to her after all. And if Harvey and the gray house would not open, then neither would all the other closed places or people—the people like Mrs. Sindles at the school, who was always so pursed-lipped and unhappy about no-one-knew-what, who were capable of doing frightening and unexpected things. They would always be that way. Nothing she could do would change it. She wept over it for a few nights, then accepted it, using one of Cloud-haired Mama's favorite phrases, ''All part of growing up.'' Disillusionment, pain, unpleasant surprise, all were part of growing up.

She became accustomed to her life: accustomed to knowing ninety-five percent of everything before it occurred; accustomed to the shock of the other five percent, the wild happenings, the accidents, unpredictable and truly frightening; the double visions that were like waking dreams; the occasional places that greeted her as though they were old friends, though Marianne could not recollect how or when they might have met.

There was a stone church at the corner of Beale Street, for example, set back a little behind a clump of trees, that spoke to her every time she saw it. ''Remember,'' it said. ''Remember?'' Its tower had an admonitory look, like a raised finger. ''Remember, Marianne. Pay attention, now.'' A massive rock shelter at the entrance to the Bitter River Road spoke in somewhat the same fashion. ''Here,'' it said. ''He has been here for some time. He will be here when needed.''

What was she to make of this? It was a mystery.

There was a small frame house where an old, old Chinese woman often lay half-asleep on the porch. When Marianne passed by, the woman spoke without opening her lips, ''One of them is inside. One you'll need, Marianne. Just keep it in mind.'' Perhaps it was not the woman who spoke at all. Perhaps it was the house that spoke.

There was a certain maple tree, bigger around than her arms would reach, which, when it was half turned yellow in the fall, whispered, "Just now, on the grass. Just this minute he's come. He's usually here. Don't forget." And a wall of Virginia creeper, bloody scarlet upon the brick, breathed, "One of them lies here every day, waiting for word from you."

Messages. From inside. Inside the church, the house, the shelter, the tree, the wall. Messages that were always delivered in the same voice. She believed the voice without understanding it at all. She did not recognize the voice although it was her own, its sound subtly changed in a way she could not have expected. It would be some time before she realized it was her own voice as an adult, as she would someday be.

Now she could only reply to the church, "No. I don't remember. I'm sorry, but I don't."

She tried to put the messages and the voice out of her mind. It was too troubling to deal with. For a year or two, she succeeded.

Until she was ten years old and had a dream.

It was very early one fall morning. She lay in her room, her arms beneath the covers, the window blowing a gauzy curtain half across her face. She was aware of this and aware at the same time that she was dreaming. In the dream, also, there was a window, but she was older, much older. An old woman, twenty or more. She sat at a desk by the window, oak twigs tapping at the panes, looking out at a green, parklike place across the street. Something horrible crouched at her feet. When she looked, it was only a box, but there was something dreadful in it. Tears dripped from her eyes onto her hands, and in the dream she knew that she grieved. She was crying because Cloud-haired Mama and Papa were dead.

She was crying because Harvey had had something to do with their deaths!

Ten-year-old Marianne sat straight up in bed, the dream as real as something she might have seen on television, a scream trembling unvoiced somewhere deep in an aching hollow inside her. They were dead. Gone. Killed. And Marianne herself was in terrible danger.

The dreamlike quality of her terror was something she

recognized within a moment. Her heart was not pounding. Her mind screamed, but her body lay upon the bed quietly, without panic. It was visionary terror, not real—or if real, not real in the way that other, more immediate things were real. Though it might hold the essence of reality, it did not exist in the here and now. It was another of those double visions, experienced this time as a dream and coming as an unmistakable warning. The message was clear and unequivocal. "If things go on as they are going," she heard that inner voice saying, "this dreadful thing will happen."

For the first time, she recognized the voice as her own.

"Who are you?" she asked, less frightened than angry that some part of her should have separated itself in this way and be playing such tricks on her.

"You know," the voice answered. "You. I am you."

"How do you know such things?" Marianne demanded aloud before she realized she did not need to vocalize for that other self to hear.

"I lived them," the voice said.

"Are you from the future?" she asked, silently.

"Perhaps," the voice said, very sadly. "In a manner of speaking. Your future is my past. I left you word, Marianne. Messages. I left you helpers. So it won't happen! You must not let it happen!"

So that was the reason for the messages. When the old stone church begged her to "remember," the word was not from this time, not from this life but from some other time, some other life in which the church had also existed. Another *Marianne* had known the church then, there. She had been inside the church, intimate with it, able to do something there, leave some symbolic taint of herself, some word, some information. Marianne the child struggled with the concept. It was as though someone had put a message in a bottle or a hollow tree, except that the message was just for her. Someone, herself, had left her a message about a terrible thing.

"Something terrible happened in that other world," she told herself. "To me. To that *Marianne*. And in this world, it must not happen. That is what the messages are all about." She was as certain of this as she was of her name. Marianne. Marianne

Zahmani. *This* Marianne. Herself.

As she lay there in bed that early morning, she worked it out, slowly. The person who had left these messages was another, a grown-up *Marianne*. She began to sense, however vaguely at first, that the life of the grown-up *Marianne* had always been there, hanging at the edges of each day's experiences, awaiting its own reaffirmation. The discovery came with a sense of shock and ultimate recognition, like seeing her face in a mirror and realizing for the first time that it was her own unique and mortal image, not an immortal shadow awaiting her in some other world. Most of her present life had simply affirmed and repeated another life! A life previously lived. By someone else! By that grown-up person that was in some strange way herself! That is why everything had been so familiar!

She had figured it out by the time people had begun to stir. She dressed for breakfast as she did every morning, not suspecting what would come next. She had not foreseen the implications of the change. Because this thing had happened that had never happened before, this morning, for the first time in her life, she went down the stairs to confront a day in which there were many events she would not foresee.

Harvey said something angry at breakfast, something she did not understand and had not anticipated. There was a guest for lunch, someone she did not recognize. By early afternoon, she was in a panic, unable to deal with this sudden, horribly surprising world. She retreated to her room, trying desperately to appear poised, failing miserably.

She felt lost, betrayed, and angry, too, at that other *Marianne* for having done this to her. Other children met the strangeness of the world as babies; by the time they were ten, they had some notion of how it was done. Now she must learn it all at once, late, without letting anyone know how hideously unprepared she was.

She learned.

Most days there were only one or two things she was not ready for. Some days were totally anticipated, just as they had always been. As she learned to poise herself upon the moment, taking her clues from others, reacting as they did, her fear and panic dwindled, but the anger remained. It was not fair to have done this to her. Not fair. Not right! Even though there was reason for the messages she had received, still, whoever-it-was shouldn't have done this to her! Shouldn't have done it even though Marianne believed that what it had told her was true.

Gradually, she came to act on that belief.

Harvey asked her to go riding with him. She remembered having done so on a bright spring morning just like this one. Now, on the morning of that day—on this morning—she decided it was better not to go.

"What's the matter, Marianne?" asked Mama. "Don't you want to go riding with your big brother?"

"No thank you, Mama. Not right now." Knowing why, precisely. That other time, in that other life, she had gone riding with Harvey and he had asked her certain questions about Mama that Marianne, all unwitting, had answered. It would be better not to talk about those things. Better not give him the opportunity to ask.

But since she did not go with him, she spent the day being terrified. By changing now what she had done in that other life, she had changed the day completely. Everything in it was different and unexpected. By evening she was exhausted at the emotional battering, and yet there was a touch of wild exhilaration as well. It had been like a roller coaster. A kind of swooping weightlessness.

Was this the way most people lived? With this shock of events? She could not decide whether she could bear it or not.

As the spring and summer wore on, the choices became more difficult and the former life increasingly unclear. Sometimes it was only possible to guess what had been done before and what kind of deviation was needed to change the old life into something new. Still, she kept trying. By August, the greater part of every day came as a surprise, and she relished the few familiar hours as rewards for the struggle she was making.

"I wish you'd girl-talk just with me, Mama. When Harvey's there, he spoils it."

"Now, Mist Princess. Harvey is your half brother. My stepson. He's family, and we have to make him feel loved and welcome." Cloud-haired Mama looked surprised and a little offended, but Marianne persevered.

"He looks at you like the man looked at the lady on TV when she took her clothes off. I just don't think he should come in your bedroom with us all the time. He makes me feel nasty."

That was not something an eleven-year-old Marianne had said the other time. Now that it had been said, however, Mama saw what Marianne had seen. What she had accepted as filial affection—Mama had very little experience of the world and Papa liked her exactly that way—could be interpreted as a much more basic emotion. Harvey was, after all, a grown man only a few years younger than Cloud-haired Mama and not of any blood kin to her. The bedroom visits were curtailed, and Marianne felt relief. That particular juncture had been safely passed.

Mama did not leave well enough alone, however. She spoke to Papa in the garden.

"Haurvatat, you should set Harvey up with his own establishment up in Boston. He's twenty-six. He's teaching full-time now, and he needs the experience of having his own establishment rather than living in hotels and commuting back and forth every weekend."

Papa agreed, somewhat surprised.

Harvey sulked, furious. "What do you and your pretty-girl mother think you're doing," he attacked Marianne. "He was my father a long time before he was yours. You think you're going to get me out of the picture, you're crazy. I'm his heir, his only son, and don't you and pretty-face forget it!"

"I don't know what you're talking about!" the child Marianne had retorted, honestly confused. "It's not nice to talk that way about Mama, Harvey."

"Papa never told me I ought to leave home until she started on him!"

"Nobody wants you to leave home. Mama just thinks you need to have a place of your own. She said I should have one, too, as soon as I'm finished with school. She says everyone needs the experience of independence."

"She's a fine one to talk."

What could Marianne say. Papa had come along and married Mama when she was only a girl. Everyone knew that. "Maybe she regrets not having had the experience, Harvey," she said in a suddenly adult voice with a mature insight, making him stare at her incredulously and coming closer to the truth than she knew.

Her feelings about all this were uncertain, vacillating. None of this had happened the other time. She didn't know what to do. There was no dream message to enlighten her, no voice coming from one of those strange places that seemed so familiar but were not. She spent long hours hiding in her bedroom or riding alone, trying to understand what needed to be done next, but there were no answers. Was Harvey being changed by her changes? Or was he doing slightly different things but remaining the same? Was the danger still there?

Her confusion was growing into something approaching a nervous collapse when an invitation arrived from Harvey's aunt, his mother's sister, Tabiti Delubovoska. Madame Delubovoska was inviting her favorite—and only—nephew for a visit in Lubovosk. A long visit.

Great-aunt Dagma had much to say about the inadvisability of this. "Tabiti is not a nice woman," she said to Papa and Mama, not seeing Marianne where she was curled behind the pillows on the window seat. "She cannot be a good influence on Harvey. She is likely to be just the opposite."

"Harvey's twenty-six," Papa said in a mild voice. "He's a grown man, Aunt Dagma. I can hardly forbid it."

"Ever since Lubovosk split away from Alphenlicht and mixed with those people from the north, there has been evil there. You know it as well as I do, Haurvatat. No good will come of this visit." She tapped her ebony cane on the floor to emphasize the point. "Mind me, nephew. No good will come of it."

Though Marianne did not remember this conversation having happened before, Harvey *had* gone to Lubovosk that other time as well. It was as though nothing had really changed! She was puzzled and anxious about this. Every time she changed something, the time pendulum swung back again. The finicky details of daily life as it had been lived before were becoming more and more vacillating and obscure, but the broad pattern seemed as though graven in stone, unchangeable.

And yet, she was grateful to see him go. With him gone, the daily pattern of life became calm, almost placid, each day's path as simple as a ribbon, running from end to end, almost totally familiar. There was danger in this placidity. Danger in the easy living of each day, danger she could feel without being able to respond to it at all. She began to wake in the middle of the night from restless dreams believing there was some message important to her that she was not receiving.

And it was in this state of frustration that she sought the Beale Street church again. Perhaps the message that had evaded her when she was a child would be clear to her now that she was twelve.

The church was usually locked. On several occasions before she had gone around it, pulling at the doors, trying to find a way in. Today, however, there had been a funeral, and the mourners were still gathered in muted clusters on the sidewalk as she slipped past them, through the open door and into the nave.

She knew it. The minute the lozenges of colored light from the tall windows began to swim across her face, she knew the place. There was a bell tower, reached by a twisting flight of stairs behind her in the corner. There was a choir loft on either side of the sanctuary, and a row of bronze plates set into the stone floor where the bodies or ashes of parishioners rested. It was, she guessed, a Catholic or Anglican church. Not a church Marianne would ever have attended. She was being taught the Magian faith of her ancient forebears, and that sect built no edifice in this place or in any other. Still, she knew this church as she knew her own bedroom. Grown-up *Marianne* had been here.

And she had left something here. The other *Marianne* had come to this place and set something here, some word, some symbol perhaps. Something meant to be found by the young Marianne in this separate life. Something to help. Here, and in the house, the shelter, the tree, the wall. In each of them was something she needed.

She sought what it held for her.

It was no message writ large in the stone. The only words carved there were ones of praise to God or thanks for past gifts. It was no song being sung. It was nothing written into the back of a hymnal. She had not really expected that.

She sat down, waiting. The place had summoned her,

"here," and she was "here," ready to listen. Time went on. The sun swam a bit lower, sending new jewels of light onto the floor and drawing her eyes up to the stained-glass window that cast them. St. George. She recognized him from a storybook. St. George and the dragon. It was not a very reptilian dragon, rather more doglike in general appearance but with a spiny crest and a lashing, lizardine tail. Its hide was blue as steel. The knight's horse was reared high in fear, and the saint looked likely to lose his seat in the instant. The spear was only a straw. The dog-dragon would bite it in two.

Sitting there in the glow brought it back. Grown-up *Marianne* had come here before, between times, to sit in this place and look at this same window. "Remember," she had whispered to the stone, the wood pews, the stained glass, the carved altar screen. "Remember," bidding them summon herself when she returned as a child, as they had done. The memory was amber, warm, glowing with satisfaction. Whatever had been done here had been done well. "Are you here?" she whispered to the window.

The dog-dragon in the stained-glass window moved its head to look at her, staring at her with large, sunflamed eyes. It panted, its pointed tongue sinuous as a serpent's. "Are you ready?" it asked. "Do you need me now?"

She gasped, wrapping her arms tightly around herself in self-protection. The dog continued to stare, its tongue flickering, an isolated shimmer of sunlight. Perhaps she was merely having another of those double visions, those bizarre transparencies laid over the reality of life. And yet, in her mind the voice seemed real and very clear, demanding an answer. "Do you need me now?"

"Not quite yet," she answered softly. "Soon, maybe."

The dog-dragon turned back to contemplate the knight poised above him, dog eyes laughing. One knew he had no fear of either the steed or the armor. When both the saint and the horse were ashes upon the wind, the dog-dragon would remain.

"He's a momentary god," a voice inside her said and was then silent. Marianne was frowning as she left the church.

Driven by a need to clarify what was happening, to connect it to anything she understood, she went to the house where the little old Chinese woman often slept upon the porch, and stood at the edge of the public walk where the brick path curved to the house. She called, tentatively, as one might call a puppy. "Here, come on, come on." Through the closed door a red dog came out, fluffed like a pom-pom, his black mouth gaped wide and his long, black tongue extended in a monstrous yawn. His face changed as she looked at it, becoming another kind of face for a moment, an Oriental face, wrinkled away from fangs much longer than any mere dog could have needed. He turned, posed, raising one foot as though to rest it upon something and she recognized him. There was a statue of him at home in Papa's room. One of him and one of his mate with a cub beneath her paw.

"Now?" he asked. "We've been reasonably patient."

"Not quite yet. I only wanted to be sure you were here."

"Where else would we be?" the dog asked with stern amusement. "Didn't you tell us to stay here until we were needed? You haven't forgotten that, have you?"

"Not really," said Marianne. "Sometimes I forget parts of things I'm supposed to know. Sometimes I get confused. I'm not always sure what's real."

"There are five of us," the dog said. "You do remember that."

"Yes," she said, surprising herself. She did know that. "I don't exactly know what all five of you are."

"You'll remember," said the red dog, turning to trot back to the porch beside the old woman. "You'll remember."

It was late and Marianne was very tired, but she did stop at the viny wall and whistle, softly, wondering what might come to her call. What came was the size of a large calf, black as the inside of a fireplace, with a mouth and eyes the color of ripe cherries, red as jelly.

"Just checking," said Marianne somewhat weakly.

"Don't waste our time, woman," the Black Dog said.

"I'm not really a woman, not yet," she said.

"Oh, yes you were," he replied. "Were, are, will be. We're ready when you are. Just call as you ride past."

"Ride past?" she asked, for that instant believing she understood everything completely. "Oh, yes. I will." She turned away, feeling the fiery eyes of the Black Dog burn into her back as she trudged home. She did not call up the dog of the shelter or the dog of the tree. Dragon Dog, Foo Dog, Black Dog—what would the others be? She was not sure she wanted to know, but her mind told her. Wolf Dog and Dingo. Blue dog, red dog, black dog, silver dog, and yellow dog.

"Momentary gods," she said to herself, remembering the words without knowing what they meant."

"Papa, what's a momentary god?" she asked him at dinner. It was safe to do so. Harvey was still abroad.

"A what, Mist Princess? A momentary god? Haven't the foggiest idea."

"Perhaps a very little god?" laughed Cloud-haired Mama. "Perhaps a very tiny one. Who only lasts for a moment?"

"Where did you hear a strange phrase like that?" Great-aunt Dagma wanted to know, cleaving immediately to the underlying significance of the question or event, as she always did. Others could be misled, or diverted by trivia, but seldom Great-aunt Dagma. "Who used those words?"

Marianne shook her head. "I don't know. I just heard it somewhere. Maybe on TV."

"I would say," Great-aunt Dagma told her, "that a momentary god is one summoned up or invoked for a momentary occasion. A brief time."

"Maybe that's it," Marianne murmured.

"I would say further," Great-aunt went on inexorably, "that anyone who did so had better have strong nerves and excellent qualities of conceptualization. I shouldn't think a momentary god would necessarily wish to be dismissed once the moment was over."

"What do you suppose one would look like?" Marianne asked, not needing to pretend innocence. She was innocent of anything except conjecture. "Do you suppose one could look like a dog?"

Great-aunt Dagma fixed her with a strange, glowing eye. "I suppose one might. Or a lion, or a multi-armed idol, or a dragon or a worm, perhaps. Depending upon what one needed."

"Tsk, Aunt Dagma, you're feeding the child stories again," Papa said.

"Well, such stories were fed to you, nephew, and you suffered little from it."

"What did you mean, Great-aunt Dagma, about the god not wanting to be dismissed?"

"Well, child. I suppose it would be like summoning a very powerful servant of some kind. Or perhaps a genie. One summons the creature up, and one says, 'Mend me that fence,' or something suitable. And the creature does it. But then, when the task is done, it does not necessarily want to go back into its bottle or to the servants' quarters where nothing interesting is happening. It may insist upon staying around, perhaps eating and drinking or chasing pretty ladies. . . ."

"Dagma!" Cloud-haired Mama cried warningly.

"Tsh, child. Marianne knows that male creatures chase pretty ladies. Even godlets or genies may do so, eh, girl? Well, that is what I meant. Not everyone has the power to put a creature of that kind back in his proper place. Perhaps it may even be hard to know what the proper place should be!"

Marianne was properly sobered by this. Evidently she, the grown-up *Marianne*, had summoned five momentary gods for some inscrutable purpose of her own. "Some necessary purpose," the adult voice inside Marianne prompted. "You'll know when the time comes." Be that as it might, the current Marianne thought very anxiously about the five great dogs. When they had done whatever it was they had been summoned up to do, what would happen then?

# CHAPTER 2

THE FAMILIAR, DREAMY time came to an end. Harvey came home from his trip to Lubovosk, bringing with him his Aunt Delubovoska who was properly invited by Cloud-haired Mama to come to tea between visits to Washington of an ambassadorial kind.

"Not that I can really think of her as an ambassador—ambassadress," Mama laughed. "Any more than I used to be able to think of my own father as one. Lubovosk and Alphenlicht are such tiny, unimportant countries, and embassies are so deadly dull. It seems to me no tiny country should need such boring places even though the great powers may have use for them. So full of maneuvering. Everything is maneuver, tactic, strategy. My own mother used to worry about the political implications of what she *wore!*"

"I'm glad Papa came along and rescued you, then," Marianne had said. "Otherwise you'd still be trapped in one."

"No." Cloud-haired Mama had been quite sad over that. "Embassy life would have ended for me when my own father died, even if Mother had lived. I would have been sent back home to Alphenlicht, I imagine. Just think of that! Being sent

18

back to a place you don't even remember and being told it's your home.''

"This is your home." Marianne had hugged her. "With Papa and me."

"Well, this has been Papa's home for a long time." Cloud-haired Mama had laughed, looking out at the wide, verdant acres. "So I guess it has to be mine as well."

"This is my home," Harvey had once said from horseback, gesturing with one arm at all the lordly expanse of it. "Mine."

"Papa's," Marianne had corrected, frightened by the gloating look in Harvey's eyes. Now, meeting Madame, Harvey's aunt, Papa's first wife's sister, Marianne saw that same look. A kind of gloating. As though everything here actually belonged to her though no one knew it just yet. This visit was a new thing. It had not happened before. So, something had changed.

"So this is Marianne," Madame Delubovoska said, smiling a brittle, terrible smile. "Little Marianne." Her eyes bored into Marianne's, questioning, demanding eyes.

Marianne felt as though she were about to choke. Her throat was swollen shut and her face was turning color. She could not breathe. Her body screamed for air.

Something moved inside her mind, as though a tenant had come into a room of it, walking very purposefully, already speaking as she entered. "I am a castle of adamant," said the voice of *Marianne* and Marianne's fist tightened in an unconscious, symbolic gesture and the choking stopped. Marianne did not fight the voice or the gesture. She relaxed to let them have their way. Madame had done something dreadful, something terribly frightening, but evidently the grown-up *Marianne* understood and was competent to do something about it, even though this had not happened in precisely this way before.

Madame looked puzzled, though only for an instant, before Papa demanded her attention. Then she turned to him, taking his hands, taking Mama's, greeting them, making some statement or other to which they both nodded agreeably. The voice inside Marianne said, "See, both of them nodding at her? They're agreeing to whatever she's saying. That puts them in her power, Marianne. In hers and in Harvey's.''

Harvey stood just behind his aunt, his eyes fixed on her every movement, strangely glittering eyes.

''Now, Marianne,'' said the voice with a sad certainty. ''It must be now. We can't wait. You see what's happening? Another day and it will be too late!''

Marianne did see. Death was in Harvey's eyes. He wanted his inheritance. He wanted it now. Or, perhaps Madame Delubovoska wanted it through him. ''Harvey,'' Marianne asked, suddenly and surprisingly, drawing all their eyes, ''will you take me riding with you in the morning?'' It was not her own voice, not her young voice, and it surprised them both. ''Please,'' she added, in her own persona, the word coming out in a childish plea, almost a whine.

''Well, of course he will!'' Madame said in a tone of devilish amusement, as though she would have chosen precisely that. ''He wouldn't miss a ride with his little sister, not for anything.'' And she turned to Harvey imperiously, the very movement a command, her eyes demanding obedience.

Then the party moved out of the lofty entryway and became only ordinary. Harvey went off to his room to unpack. Madame had tea with Mama and Papa in the library. She would stay, she said, only for an hour. Then she must go. It was all very civilized, and Marianne sat with them, sipping her own tea, cold as ice inside herself where that other *Marianne* watched and watched. ''You see,'' said the adult *Marianne* voice. ''Look at her!''

Marianne looked, seeing something horrible in the woman's eyes. Pain and terror for Mama, first, then for Papa, and perhaps, at last, for Marianne herself. ''You see!'' the voice demanded.

''Mama, may I be excused?'' she begged, sweat standing out on her forehead. ''Please.''

''What's the matter, Princess? Not feeling well?'' Mama saw something in Marianne's eyes, for she asked no more questions. ''Run on. I'll be up to see you in a moment.''

And so she had escaped, she and that other she both, to go up to Marianne's room and sit crouched over the windowsill, leaning out into the quiet airs of early fall. The voice spoke to her. "It's all right. Listen, Marianne. It will all be taken care of."

"What am I to do?" she asked that other person, that grown-up voice. "Tell me, what am I to do?"

"Go riding with Harvey," the voice said. "Go past the church, the house, the tree, the wall, the shelter, then on up Bitter River Road, into the forest. That's all. I summoned the momentary gods to help you, and they will take care of it."

Was this real? She couldn't tell. "That's all I have to do. Nothing other than that?"

"Everything else has been arranged."

Marianne began to cry.

"Shhh, shhh," the voice comforted her. "Shhh. I'm sorry, dear one. I'm sorry little Marianne. Sorry to treat you so, use you so. But Cloud-haired Mama will die, otherwise. Papa will die. Madame and Harvey will choke the life out of them in just the way she was testing on you when she first came in, to see if you were vulnerable. Then, when Mama and Papa are dead, they'll take years to do the same to me, you, us."

"Why? Why?" She knew why. It was a plea for sympathy rather than for information, but the voice replied as though she had not really known.

"Why? For money, little girl. For all these lands and the money in the bank, Papa's, Mama's. There is more of it than you can imagine, and much of it will go to Harvey when they die. But a lot of it comes to you, Marianne, to you, me, us, and if we die, it goes to charity. Good works. Feed the hungry, rock the baby, build the hospital. You know, Marianne. Not to Harvey. But he is a trustee! So, he won't do us in, not just yet. Later. When he's had a chance to use it all up."

"And she . . . that aunt of his, she's in on it?"

"Why, Marianne, she's *it*. She's taught him everything he knows."

"What does she want?"

"The money, Marianne. Money is power. Lubovosk is a poor little country, and she needs money. Papa is very, very wealthy. Once Harvey has it, she has him. She will siphon it off, through him. He thinks he can do what he pleases. She knows he will do only what she allows."

Marianne didn't understand it. She knew about greed and desire for money. For power. But she couldn't believe anyone would kill Mama for it. Or Papa. And yet, she had looked deep into Madame's eyes. After that, anyone would believe.

"All I have to do is go riding?"

"That's all you have to do."

She could not really know whether any part of this was real, and the unreality persisted through the night and into the morning as she put on her riding clothes and boots, as she greeted her horse at the stable where Harvey awaited her. "Well, where do you want to ride, little sister?" He had a narrow, superior grin on his face, like a fox's face, gleeful and anticipatory. "I thought we'd go along the forest path if it's all right with you."

"No," the voice said.

"No," said Marianne. "I want to ride by the edge of town and out the Bitter River Road."

He stared at her, one nostril lifted in scorn, somewhat angrily, as though wondering how important it was to do what she wanted. Abruptly, he decided it didn't matter. He mounted, not waiting for her, and trotted down the driveway to the road. Reluctantly, Marianne mounted Rustram and followed him, Rustram hopping and curveting to attract her attention. She patted him absently, adrift half in fatalistic resolve, half in terror.

The road into town was only half a mile from their gates, and Marianne saw the blue Dragon Dog waiting at the intersection, the stone steeple of the church spiking the sky behind him like a raised cudgel. "Shh," said the voice. "Ride on."

It was a dream, she told herself. A waking dream.

The maple tree was on the way, and the yellow Dingo Dog came out of it as she passed, nose first, then ears and neck, finally the upcurving tail, out through the bark as though it had been a curtain of gauze, trotting along behind as though it had followed Marianne every day when she rode. The wall was next, and Black Dog rose from the Virginia creeper at its base to pace along beside them. "Good morning," he said to her silently. "I'm glad you've finally gotten around to it."

"Shhh," said the voice again.

"I think I see Bitter River Road from here," Harvey said. "There's a shortcut across the meadow."

"No," said Marianne. "I need to see something at the end of this block." She must dream this thing as she had been told, even though it wasn't real.

"You're becoming very unaccommodating, I must say," Harvey sneered. "Though you've grown up amazingly while I've been gone. Almost as pretty as your mama. Might be worth kissing, Marianne, pet. Think I'll test that when we get home."

Marianne stared at him, cold in her belly. "No," she said. "You won't." Dream or not, she didn't want him to touch her.

He laughed, reaching out to stroke her chest where her breasts were just beginning to swell. "Oh, won't we?"

She shuddered away from him as they passed the house of the old Chinese woman, and the Foo Dog came from under the porch, high as her armpit and red as a flower pot. "One more," the red dog said conversationally. "Only one more."

"I know," said Marianne, aloud.

"Did you say something, little sister?" Harvey asked.

"Not to you," said Marianne. They went on down the road. The shelter lay on the left, a vast rockpile built during WPA days, with a fanciful roof and a great chimney up the middle. At one time it had been used as a site for picnics, but no one used it any more. Ferns grew in crevices among the stones. The entrance was blocked by a forest of burdock, and the Wolf Dog came through the leaves as though they were smoke. She was silver in the sunlight, glittering. Her plumy tail waved a greeting and she looked at Marianne out of eyes like great amber lamps.

"All here," said Black Dog.

"All here," agreed the Dragon Dog and the Foo Dog.

"Hmmm," growled the wolf, deep in her throat.

The Dingo was silent, sneaking looks at the others out of the sides of her eyes.

Marianne touched Rustram with her heels and he sprang obediently into a canter along the dirt road. She did not know where they were going, but someone did. She did not need to look at them to know the five momentary gods were keeping easy pace. In the shapes that other *Marianne* had assigned to them? Or in their own shapes? Which?

"Come back here you little witch," Harvey shouted, irritated. He wasn't as good a rider as Marianne. Horses didn't like him, and in any case, his horse was no match for Rustram. Both these things annoyed him, and he clattered after her, furious at being outrun. She fled on, the dogs tight at her heels, around the curve of the River Road and under a huge oak that stood in a clutter of boulders at the forest's edge.

"Stop here," the voice said.

"Here," said several of the momentary gods, all at once.

She stopped, turned, waited to see what would happen.

Harvey rode toward her, his face crimson with anger, his whip hand raised. He got angry easily. Perhaps he would whip his horse. Perhaps he would whip her. He had not decided when the dogs erupted from the underbrush and were suddenly all around him. A pack of curs, he thought, mongrel whelps appearing out of the underbrush all in a moment. One of them, a large, gray one, leaped for the throat of his horse. Another caught at his ankle, tearing him from his seat. It was the huge, black one that caught his hand, the one holding the whip, and jerked him off of the horse, down. He put out his other hand to protect himself from the rock he saw beneath him. Too late.

He felt the rock hit the back of his head, crushingly.

He was not unconscious.

He could still see. She was sitting on her horse, staring at him. At him. Not at the dogs. The dogs. Sitting around her, looking at him also. Licking their mouths. A yellow one burrowing into its shoulder as though for a flea.

"They're yours," he said in a whisper. "Yours."

"Not mine," she shook her head. "Not mine, Harvey." It was all a dream. Her pulse was not fast. There was no feeling about it. He lay there and she was not even glad, not even sorry. She dreamed she said, "You and your aunt shouldn't have planned to kill Mama and Papa. You really shouldn't have."

"How did you find out? Bitch," he snarled. It was the last word he ever said. Something beneath him broke. He felt an abrupt, almost painless cracking in his neck, and then all feeling ceased.

\* \* \*

"What now?" she whispered. Perhaps she would wake up, now.

"Ride home, very fast, and tell them what happened," said her voice.

She rode. She told them. Dogs, she said, for that is what she had seen. She said they had come out of the forest, jumped at Harvey, pulled him from his horse. All of that was true, and the horror in her voice needed no pretense. She was horrified at Harvey and at herself and even at the sorcerous voice that spoke from deep inside herself. The real anger at that voice was yet to come.

# CHAPTER 3

THERE WERE PHONE CALLS, ambulances, men with a stretcher. There were low-voiced conversations with doctors. Later, there was a hunt for the dogs by an armed posse, but the animals had vanished as though they had never existed.

"Can you describe them?" the animal control officer asked Marianne. "How many were there?"

"Five. I counted five," she said.

"You said one big black one."

"Very big. And one that looked like a wolf. And a red one. And a smaller yellow one. And one that was kind of bluish."

"Bluish?" Papa asked, unbelieving.

The animal control officer did not disbelieve. "Well, yes sir, it could be. A blue tick hound, maybe. They're really sort of dark gray with white mixed in. It does look bluish, particularly in the sun."

"Does her description mean anything to you?"

"I'm afraid not. Dogs will pack, of course. It's as natural to them as—well, as going to football games is to us. Usually when we hear about a pack, it's made up of dogs from adjacent properties. They get acquainted along their borders, so to speak, and then they run together when they get the chance. It

26

doesn't take much to make a friendly pack into a hunting pack, either. That's natural to dogs, too, but I've never heard of a pack attacking a mounted man." He fell silent, musing for a time before he went on, "I know of one big black dog, but he's old as the hills and almost toothless. As for the rest of them, well, it's an odd assortment, you'll admit. You sure about the colors and sizes, Marianne?"

"Yes sir." She was. She could even have told the officer where to find the dogs, but he hadn't asked her that. When she thought it over, she realized he could not have found them there, even if she had told him.

"How about breeds. Do you know anything about different breeds of dog?"

"The red one was like the dog in Papa's office."

They went into the office to look at the pair of Foo Dogs on Papa's desk: the male, on the right, with his foot upon the globe; the female, on the left, with her foot upon her pup.

"What are they, sir? Some kind of idol?"

"Temple guardians," Papa had replied. "If they look like any living breed at all, I'd say it would be the chow. That would go with the red coloring Marianne mentioned. Chows have black mouths and tongues, too."

"His mouth was black," said Marianne, verifying the identification. This, too, was perfectly true.

Papa raged and the animal control man sympathized, but they didn't find the pack of dogs.

"What now?" she asked her internal voice, still dreaming. None of it was real. Not any of it.

"Now?" The voice was remote, as though it reached her from some incredible distance. "Marianne; nothing now. You've saved them. You've saved yourself. Now you must get on with your life and they must go on with theirs."

"That's *all!*" She was incredulous.

"That's all." The sadness in that voice! Marianne was too young to recognize the components of that emotion—aching love and a piercingly sweet renunciation—but she could not miss the sadness. "Oh," the voice went on, with tears in it, "except one thing. When you are about twenty-one or -two, maybe a little older than that, you may meet a man. His name is Makr Avehl. He comes from Alphenlicht, like I—like we do. He may know all about this. About Harvey, everything. He's—he's a very—well, he's a very good friend of ours.''

"Do you—do you love him?'' In the vision, it seemed appropriate that she should love him.

"He saved my life. He loves me,'' the voice said sadly. "I do love him. I don't know if you will or not.'' It went away then. Purposefully and absolutely, as though some tenuous line that had tied it to this Marianne had been deliberately severed and the connection between them had been broken. Young Marianne knew that grown-up *Marianne* was gone. Not merely elsewhere, but gone. There were no longer two, but only one. If the other *Marianne* had been correct about Madame and about Harvey, no one knew it now except young Marianne herself. And perhaps the man. Makr Avehl. If he were real and not merely part of the dream.

"Mack Ravel,'' she said to herself, already forgetting the name. "From Alphenlicht.''

Time went on. The motionless body that was Harvey came home from the hospital with two attendants and a wheeled litter. His attendants said he could see well enough. He could even signal yes and no by blinking his eyes, though he seemed to do so only in response to questions concerning food or temperature. Would he like more ice cream? Was it too warm? The eyes would blink—once for yes, twice for no. If one asked anything unrelated to food or temperature, "Would you like to go out on the lawn, Harvey?'' there was no response at all.

Sometimes she would come into a room and find him parked there, just lying, looking at her. Sometimes she saw something in his silent stare that could not really be there, something smoldering, like flame beneath a pile of ashes. She told herself it was only because she needed to see something rather than this vacancy. In reality, everyone said there was nothing there. The doctors agreed. The body lived, but whatever had been Harvey within it did not.

Seeing him thus helpless, unmanned, dehumanized, converted into something that was kept alive only out of a conventional sense of the appropriate, made her former belief in the immediacy of danger seem remote and unlikely. The precarious world of her dream-threat faded; her conviction went with it. She did not really believe in it. Belief in the momentary gods departed. She did not think they had really existed, either. By the time she was fourteen, fifteen, she knew that none of it had been real. The accident had been only an accident. There had been dogs. Only dogs. The rest was woven out of fairy tales and too much imagination and an overbred sense of guilt. Her childhood had not really been as she remembered it, all known ahead of time. There had not really been a grown-up *Marianne* in her head. All those double visions of things had not actually happened. They had resulted from some kind of juvenile nervous disorder, now outgrown. She did not tell herself it would never happen again. She merely thought of it as an aberration, one she could handle.

All her memories shifted, changed, underwent a softening as she told herself what she had thought was real had been only a childish imagination.

Until at last there was nothing left at all. Except, from time to time, a feeling of formless guilt. Try though she might to tell herself that it had only been an accident, something inside accused her of being responsible for Harvey's condition. His silent body became ubiquitous, a constant accusation. He seemed to inhabit every room of the house simultaneously. He and the litter were inseparable, half living, half mechanical, not a life but an accusatory device. She twisted beneath the pressure of guilt, feeling it a burden that she longed to shift away from herself.

Who had done it really?

That other *Marianne* who was only a fiction? Fictions cannot be responsible for anything.

Was there a real person involved in all this? She would wait and see. If there was, that person was surely responsible for whatever had happened. If anything had happened.

"It wasn't my fault," some childish part of her continued to insist. "I didn't do anything. If anybody did anything at all, they did it."

\* \* \*

Time went. School went. Out of her love for her horse and her interest in animals of all kinds, out of her devotion to the vast acres that Papa Zahmani had said one day would be hers, she had studied agriculture and livestock and business management, knowing she would have to prove herself to Papa before he would let her, a woman, manage the estate with its huge stables of thoroughbreds and its herds of purebred cattle. Papa would never have considered her if Harvey had been well and able, but Harvey wasn't. Guilt bit at her again, but she shrugged it off and went on with her studies.

The University went. There was a love affair, sweet and intense and sudden as a summer shower, over as soon, leaving Marianne wondering what she had seen in a particular egotistic, not very interesting, and totally predictable young man. With encouragement from Mama, she decided to forget him by visiting the land of her forebears. She spent several happy weeks among the small villages of Alphenlicht, picking up a little of its language and learning of its customs, no stranger to her than others she had seen in places far closer. When she read of the Prime Minister of the country, Makr Avehl, it was with a sense that she might have read or heard the name before, but it made no particular impression. The papers said he was on his way to the United Nations in New York. There was another dispute between Alphenlicht and neighboring Lubovosk. Madame Delubovoska had asserted a right for Lubovosk to govern the lands of Alphenlicht. The Prime Minister ridiculed these specious claims. The matter would be heard before the general assembly. Reading of this, Marianne experienced a tremor of recollection, as though, after a long detour, she had come once again upon an old, well-traveled road. The sensation lasted only for a moment. Real memories did not form; no voice spoke.

She went home again. It was time to get on with her life. Time to take a job. Time to become herself.

She waited, deciding among several job offers, spending a lot of time riding to use up recurrent spasms of nervous energy. She felt she should be doing something, fighting some battle, accomplishing some task she could not define even for herself. Something. Something quite remarkable.

Until the afternoon she rode up to the house and found Papa

and Mama on the terrace, entertaining a tall, spectacularly handsome man. She had seen his picture often in Alphenlicht. She recognized him with disbelief, wondering what had brought him here, accepting the introduction to him as she would to any total stranger.

"And you are Marianne," said Makr Avehl.

She, wondering what he was doing here, gave him her usual glowing smile, which he misinterpreted at once.

During dinner they exchanged only pleasantries, slightly formally as was consistent with their just having met. Great-aunt Dagma gave them both a long, level look through her glasses but said nothing. Marianne felt herself flush under that look and resented it. When dinner was done, he asked her to walk with him in the garden.

"Marianne," he said to her as soon as they were out of sight of the terrace, drawing her close to him. "Oh, by all that's holy, my Marianne."

"What in hell!" she exclaimed, breaking away from him and turning as though to flee, stopping only at his shout of half pain, half dismay. She was angrier than she could have thought possible. "I don't know you," she grated at him. "What do you think you're doing?"

He stood there, trembling, unable to speak, staring at her, searching her face for the woman he remembered. In his own memory, he had left *Marianne* only days before—or rather, had been left by her—in a strange, sorcerous world she had helped to create. She had left him there, but he had found her again—except that he seemed to have found a different woman.

The difference was there, in her face. This was not the gallant *Marianne* who played life's deck even when it was stacked against her. This woman was no less lovely but far less tried. There was little or no pain in this one's face. Perhaps this one had courage also, but it might well be of a different kind. Except for a shadow of guilt, this one had clear, untroubled eyes. They might have been sisters. Even twins. But not the same.

"Accept my apology," he said from an agonized throat. "I truly thought—never mind what I thought. Forgive me. Pretend it didn't happen." He turned away, then back to her as though he could not leave her and she responded to the pain in his face as she had not to his importunity. "Walk with me," he said at last in a voice aching with loss, needing to move before he froze into place, turned into ageless ice by this grief he felt.

She wanted to refuse him but could not do so without being ungracious. He had obviously made a mistake. Perhaps he had known someone else by her name, someone with the family resemblance. He, himself, might have been her father's son or younger brother. She had no wish to be rude, though she could not help being angry. The latter was understandable, but the former was beneath her. So Cloud-haired Mama often said. So she thought. He was not being demanding. A little resentfully but graciously enough she turned to walk beside him on the path while he examined her face as though it had been a holy icon of his religion.

"You really don't remember?" he asked in a voice pathetically pleading for such a big and powerful man. "You really don't."

"I don't know what you're talking about, Your Excellency."

"There was—there was another *Marianne*. Your twin. You, in another world. She—I . . . I loved her very much."

She softened at his tone. It would have been impossible not to. One would not kick the victim of an accident, someone lying broken on the road. So, she could not kick at him emotionally when he was so obviously broken.

"It's odd you should speak of another *Marianne*," she murmured. "When I was a child, I sometimes thought there was another *Marianne*. Although I know now it was only hallucination, it seemed then I had a grown-up twin, in my head, somewhere. An older self. At one time I bothered myself a lot trying to figure out whether she was real."

"What if I told you she was?"

Wary, she responded, "I don't care. It wouldn't have anything to do with me. I seem to remember that from the time I was about five until about twelve, there was a voice inside me, a kind of prompter. It may have been imaginary. At the time, it seemed to tell me things. Things that were going to happen." A sudden and unexpected memory assailed her, "It told me your name."

"Yes," he prompted.

"It's hard to . . . think of that time."

"The voice told you about your half brother, and Madame Delubovoska?"

She looked at him in shock, suddenly awash in memory, long repressed. She gasped. It had not occurred to her he would know what the voice had said. How could anyone in this real world know what her own delusions had spoken of? She dithered, muttering, "Some things about them, yes. I'd rather not think about that, if you don't mind."

The guilt that haunted her from time to time was manifest in her voice, and he reached out to her. "Let me verify what the voice told you."

"Your Excellency, I've dealt with that. I've forgotten it. I don't want to hear."

"You must hear. There's pain in your voice. Whatever happened, you feel involved. Your involvement bothers you. In this world, your act, whatever it was, does not seem to be self defense. It must seem to you to be almost gratuitous violence. Your generous nature would repudiate such violence. It would revulse you. What can I say to counter your revulsion if not to tell you what you did was justified?

"In my world, that other world, the one you don't remember, there was a girl named Marianne Zahmani. She called her mother Cloud-haired Mama. Her mother died when she was thirteen years old. No one knew why. No one could find out why or how except that she seemed to have choked to death. About a year later, Marianne's father died. Again, no one knew why or how. Both of them seemed to choke to death, but the doctors couldn't find any reason for it. Marianne's half brother was left as Marianne's guardian and as executor of Marianne's estate. My sister believes he may have tried to seduce her sexually when she was still only a child; certainly he did everything in his power to bend her to his will, to destroy her spirit. Finally, when he had diverted most of her inheritance for his own purposes, he decided to kill her."

"No," she snarled at him. It wasn't fair for him to drag this dream stuff out into the light. "I don't want to know. . . ."

"You have to know. He decided to kill her. He tried to kill

her as he had killed her mother and his own father, he and his
aunt, Madame Delubovoska. They used—well, call it sorcery. I
came along and spoiled things for them. So, they removed her
from my influence. See—I do not say 'you,' I say 'her.'" He
paused, struggling with the word. He said it. He still could not
accept it. "They took her into another world, a false dream
world. I pursued her there, with Aghrehond, *Marianne's* friend,
Aghrehond. We helped her escape into still another world, one
of her own. Madame and Harvey followed her there. So did my
friend, so did I. She escaped again, back into her own past.
Working with herself as a child, with you as a child, somehow
she has changed things."

Marianne turned away, angry once again. He was bringing it
all back, all the confusion and pain, giving it reality, status.
"I'll assume for one moment you knew some other *Marianne*
though I don't believe it. I'll assume it for your sake, because
you believe it. If this woman mixed into my life, she had no right
to. I've thought it over and over. Doing that to a child is like
molesting a baby. Childhoods should be sacrosanct. Children
have a right to innocence, to discovery! Assume she reached
back into *her* childhood, assume that. Well, it was *my* childhood
she ruined. Destroyed." Her voice burned with the disinterment
of a long-buried resentment. "She did it to me."

She heard her own voice in disbelief. Did she really believe
this nonsense? "That is, she—she did it to me if she existed. I
don't really believe she did."

He stared at her with a skeptical look. "Would you rather
have seen your parents die?"

"I have only your word for that. And hers. How do I know
that's true?"

"You have my word," he said stiffly, almost angrily. "What
Makr Avehl says is true is true."

"So you say. In this world it didn't happen. Or perhaps it
never happened. Perhaps the whole thing is illusion, a shared
illusion between you and her. I don't know. I don't pretend to
know. I don't want to know."

"But she talked to you!"

"Someone seemed to, yes, Makr Avehl. Then. The last thing

she said to me was that you might come. And that she loved you.'' She told him this reluctantly, but in a sense he was owed at least this.

"Love me. Oh, *Marianne*, to hear that you love me . . .''

"No, no,'' she waved him away, hands out, voice hostile. *"She.* Not me. She. The other *Marianne*. A ghost. A dream we shared, perhaps. She doesn't exist. I wish you could agree with me that she probably never did.''

It took him some time to control himself, but he did. When he turned toward her again it was with a stern, calm face.

"Tell me what happened to your half brother?''

She told him what she had decided to remember. "An accident, that's all. I think there was a pack of dogs and an accident.''

"A pack of dogs?''

"At the time I thought they were something else,'' she laughed. "I called them momentary gods. I was very confused as a child.''

He shook his head, staring into the distance, not looking at her because it was too painful to do so, musing almost to himself. "So. She was thoughtful of you, Marianne. You didn't actually have to do anything, did you? There is no need for you to feel guilt. She did it, not you. She had it all arranged through the momentary gods. When it was all over, how did you dismiss them?''

"I'm sure they were imaginary. They dismissed themselves. Things we imagine as children disappear when we become older.''

He became very pale, though she could not see it in the equally pallid light of the cloud-shifted moon. "Did she? The—my *Marianne*. Did she dismiss them?''

"I have no idea. Funny. My Great-aunt Dagma had something to say about dismissing gods. I've forgotten what it was.''

His voice was tense. She disliked the sound of it, the way it made her feel. Something inside her responded to his tension with a twanging discordancy of its own. "And what about Harvey's aunt?'' he asked. "My cousin. Madame Delubovoska? Have you seen her? Heard of her?''

"Nothing. She called when she heard Harvey had been hurt. She sent flowers to the hospital. I remember Mama calling it 'conventionalized concern.' She never came to see him."

"He was of no more use to her then. Which doesn't mean she may not still be very interested in your family, Marianne. And in you."

"Why? She's no kin to me. To Papa's first wife and to Harvey, yes, not to me. What possible reason could she have to be concerned with me?"

Makr Avehl could think of at least one very good reason, and he started to tell her but she wasn't listening to him. She was wondering, at that moment, whether he and the other *Marianne* had been lovers. Her own prurient curiosity offended her, and she answered his comment with annoyance. Something about the family fortunes. "I know very little about Papa's affairs," she said coldly. "It certainly isn't something I should discuss with someone who is virtually a stranger."

He was silent for a long time. Their feet made parallel tracks across the grass, wet with evening dew. The scent of flowers blew into their faces. Behind them the lights of the house fell across the paved terraces in long, elegant fingers of colorless light.

"If I tell you you are in danger, you will not believe me," he said at last, rather stiffly. "You are not the woman I loved, not the woman who loved me. And yet, you are." He stared at her. "Perhaps there is someone else in your life?"

"No," she said, intrigued despite herself. She did not want to be taken for someone else, but how could she mind being sought as herself? Certainly any woman would find this man's attentions flattering. "No, Makr Avehl, there isn't anyone else. But I'm not the woman you loved or thought you loved, and you have to accept that. I'm really not."

She said it. He was facing her as she said it, his eyes fixed on hers. Her voice was clear and cold. And yet, somewhere behind her eyes a shadow slipped along, like the shadow of a lonely inhabitant in a house tenanted by others, peering through a half-curtained window at a world she could not reach.

He gasped. There, in that shadow, had been something he

had recognized. Gallantry in the tilt of a head. Courage in the slope of a shoulder. He tried to contrive some way to maintain his contact with her and with that lonely, embattled shadow. He spoke, pleadingly.

"In the normal way, I might simply try to become better acquainted with you, believing that you and she are not so unalike that I could not—" he paused, struggling to find words she would not resent or think patronizing, "—could not show you something of myself you would consider . . . acceptable. I would take my time about it, as I tried to do before. But—but I erred before. Even though I knew my *Marianne* was in great danger, I didn't warn her, didn't guard her. She was shy of me, and I didn't want to frighten her. Well, you are not shy, but even if you were, I would have to warn you. I believe you are still in danger from Madame Delubovoska."

"Me?" She laughed, shaking her head, believing his sincerity though she totally disbelieved what he said. "Surely not!"

"Yes. I believe you are in danger from her."

"You think Madame remembers what you say happened?" She was intrigued by this thought. How many people in the world might remember that other *Marianne?* How many did it take to give a figment life?

"I don't know. Your parents don't remember. They wouldn't. My *Marianne* and you were virtually identical up until the time . . . the time your parents died in one life, lived in another. There was no dissonance, not for them. Probably only I and some of the other Kavi remember it at all. Because we knew that *Marianne,* and followed her to—to you."

"Kavi?"

"Our people. Our class. In Alphenlicht. The rulers. The Magi."

"Our class."

"I include you, Marianne. Because of who your parents are."

"Oh, yes. I remember now. You are a Magus! I'd forgotten that. I visited Alphenlicht. It's a pretty country. Like all the better parts of an older century. I have the feeling you should go back there and forget all the ghosts, Makr Avehl." She laughed, unconvincingly. "As I'm going to try to do. For the first eleven or twelve years of my life, I remember that every movement seemed to be foreordained. I don't think I resented it then, but I've definitely resented it since. You are the last thing connected with that time. I suppose I've been subconsciously waiting to see whether you showed up before . . .''

"Yes? Before what?"

"I don't know. Before being something completely of my own, I think."

"But not with me?"

"That's not an appropriate question." A part of her wanted to end the whole relationship, to say something final, but he was already too hurt to wound further without reason. "You're a man I would love to know better under other circumstances, but I need to feel I have choices. I've not had many up until now."

"You wouldn't consider staying close by me? Letting me protect you?"

She gave him a critical glance, shaking her head. He knew better. "That's no choice! It's just more of the same. Having you beside me, directing me, is just like having that imaginary voice inside me, directing me! Listen to me! I'm talking as though all that time was real, even though I've known since I was fifteen it was all invention and fantasy."

"It wasn't imaginary," he shook his head. "I'm not the kind of person to fall in love with phantasms."

"I'm sorry," she said again. For an instant she wanted to comfort him. She still had angry feelings about him, but they seemed less substantial when directed at a real person than when she had merely imagined him. "Perhaps sometime I'll visit you. I've been in Alphenlicht and liked it. Perhaps sometime you will visit me. But I can't—won't—make commitments. Not now!''

He sighed again, searching her face. A little willful, that face. Willfulness was easy to understand, however. She had only been exercising her will in recent years. And behind that facade, something more complex. Hidden. Why hidden? Was that other presence hiding from him?

Sad and lost as he was, he had to accept what she told him. He started to bid her good-bye, then stopped himself. "Oh, by the way. I have a gift for you. From my sister, Ellat. She was very fond of . . . of *Marianne*. I forgot to bring it with me today. If you don't mind, I'll drop it off before leaving for home.''

She assented. He was going. Let him do whatever he needed to do to put this behind him. Let him return briefly on the following afternoon. So—her independence was postponed for a day. She could bear it. She watched him go with a sense of a milestone being passed.

He returned, as he had promised. Before going inside to make his farewells to her parents, Makr Avehl introduced her to Aghrehond. Or, reintroduced her, according to Aghrehond.

''Oh, pretty lady, what a consternation and unhappiness you have put upon us. He, the Prime Minister, is cast down, but I—I am shattered.''

''Why shattered, Aghrehond?''

''That you should have forgotten the perils we shared.'' He regarded her with sad brown eyes, his chins quivering and his large stomach swaying from side to side in an excess of grief, like a bell, silently tolling. ''We had considered everything but this. That you would hate my master for the forms he had taken. . . .''

''I really don't know what forms he may have taken, Aghrehond. You'll have to accept that I honestly know nothing about it.''

''Accept, of course. One accepts. One raises one's fists to the heavens and cries woe, but one accepts. We had considered some putative hatred you might have felt, and had accepted that. We had considered that you might, in your re-growing, so to speak, have found someone else, younger and more charming than is Makr Avehl. We had considered—oh, I will not weary you with the catalogue of considerations. This single thing we had not considered. That you had forgotten. Oh, to be forgotten! Like a lost shoe, missing even its mate, in the corner of some vast closet of time!''

Despite herself, she laughed. ''It's hard for me to believe I've met you before, Aghrehond. You would be very hard to forget.''

''There! You see! It is as I told the Prime Minister. Him, you might forget. What is he after all but a very powerful, magical, charming and very handsome man. But I, Aghrehond, I am unique!''

''Yes, but you see, that very fact proves my point. I didn't remember, not even you. Therefore, Makr Avehl must accept the fact that I don't remember him, either.''

''Oh, he accepts, pretty lady. I accept. His sister, Ellat, who loved you like a daughter almost, she accepts. The Kavi of the Cave of Light shake their heads and write the whole thing down in their chronicles, adding to their lectionaries, and even they accept. So? What good is it, this acceptance? What are we to do with it?''

She shook her head, confused. ''Do with it?''

''Well, yes. What are we to do with this acceptance? Go away and forget you? Stay here and annoy you? It is much of a problem, this acceptance. Believe me!'' He wiped his brow on which small beads of perspiration glittered, running his hands over his head and around his large ears, as though to assure himself head and ears were in their proper shape.

''What form did he take?'' Marianne asked, suddenly curious. ''Makr Avehl, I mean.''

''Whatever it was, you may be assured it was appropriate to the occasion.''

''But what was it?''

He shook his head. ''My master says I talk too much. This is true, by the way, my only failing. It comes from having a hyperactive imagination and, for that reason, must be tolerated. My imagination is often very helpful.''

He wouldn't say more than that. However, that conversation had done what Makr Avehl's piteous looks had not. It had made Marianne curious about what had happened, and curiosity is a powerful stimulant. Even Marianne would have admitted that her curiosity about Makr Avehl as a sexual man had definitely been stirred.

Just before he left, Makr Avehl fished in his pocket and brought forth a length of chain, heavy gold links from which a dangling crystal hung in a pendant of gold, sparkling even in the dim light.

"Will you wear this, please?"

"What is it?"

"Call it a talisman. As I mentioned, a gift from my sister, Ellat."

"If it isn't . . . isn't meant as any kind of tie. . . ."

He laughed, a harsh, ugly sound. "An engagement present, perhaps? Like a ring? Hardly, Marianne. Ellat sent it because she is fond . . . was fond of you. The other you. You see, she remembers."

"I'm sorry," she murmured. "I didn't mean . . ."

"Wear it to give pleasure to someone you do not remember. And because it's a pretty thing." He patted her gently on one shoulder, almost an avuncular caress. She had no idea what that casual contact cost him in self control. He sighed, "And I will get myself off to keep from distressing you further. So it must be, I think, with victims of amnesia. They do not remember, and all their loved ones undoubtedly gather around insisting that they do. 'Do you remember that time we?' they ask. 'Remember old so-and-so, who . . .' And of course the poor victims do not remember. . . .

"Perhaps the relatives and friends believe the victim is only pretending not to remember, or that he would remember if he put his mind to it. I detect in myself a desire to shake you and demand that you do remember. Perhaps it is the same with the very old who forget everyone around them, mixing the generations, calling their grandchildren by the names of people long dead."

"But it doesn't seem like that to me. I don't have any missing parts in my life at all. I can account for every day, every hour!" She stepped back from him, wearying of the argument. She wanted him to go.

"Lucky Marianne. For me it now seems that my whole life is missing. May I write to you here?"

"Temporarily. I'll be leaving home shortly. I'm taking a job!"

"I see."

"With the government. Out west."

"What is 'out west,' in your lexicon?"

"Well, it happens to be Colorado. The State of. A lot of the federal bureaus have offices there, the Department of Agriculture among them."

"It is very mountainous there, I believe. Like Alphenlicht."

"Mountainous, yes, but only down the middle. The east side is very flat."

"And what will you do there?"

"I will be working for the Department of Agriculture as a consultant, a minor functionary. My specialty is livestock. I'm supposed to be able to teach people how to make money at raising stock of various kinds."

He laughed. "I'm sorry, Marianne. But it is so incongruous. I can see you among horses, yes, and dogs. But I balk at sheep and cows."

"And goats and pigs," she said firmly. "Also chickens, turkeys, and perhaps llamas and buffalo. There is a growing market for both llamas and buffalo. Perhaps I will send you a pair of young llamas to use as pack animals on your treks in the mountains of Alphenlicht."

"Perhaps you would bring them."

"Perhaps." She smiled. It was not a promise, but neither was it a rejection.

"You will be living where?"

"Denver, for now. Or one of the suburbs. I'll take an apartment temporarily. I'll look for an old house to remodel. I've got this thing for houses, preferably old ones." She stopped for a moment, aware of a memory tugging at her that she couldn't quite place. She shrugged mentally and went on. "I've always wanted to remodel one for myself."

Makr Avehl started to speak, then shut his mouth. She had already remodeled an old house in that other life, but she wouldn't know that. He remembered the Italianate Victorian house just opposite the University campus, the rosy brick, the oak leaves unfurling like tiny hands outside the window. The place where his *Marianne* had lived. It was a ruin, now, gutted. Someone was tearing it down to build an apartment building on the site. He didn't mention it.

"Will you write and give me your address?"

"If you like. When I have one."

"Farewell, pretty lady," said Aghrehond, irrepressibly. "Do not let us become strangers again."

She saw them go with strangely mixed feelings. Half was regret. Half was an ebullient joy, a jerk of release, like a spring let go. She was flung into anticipation. All the ties to her childhood dream life were gone. Now, once and for all, she could be herself.

# CHAPTER 4

"WHAT I DON'T understand," said Ellat, her forehead wrinkled in concentration, "is how you can remember everything and she remembers nothing!"

Makr Avehl shook his head, took another sip of his morning coffee, and rose to walk to the window where he looked down across the fields that surrounded the Residence to the bordering woods of Alphenlicht and the road that joined that tiny country to the outer world. "I've tried to figure it out myself," he said. "Most simply, I am the same person. She is not. My *Marianne* was driven by powerful emotions. Rage. Fear. Both combined. She went out of the dream-world into another world, the world of her own past."

"According to Nalavi and many of the other Kavi, that would have caused an alternative world."

"Well, it didn't. My *Marianne* went back in her own world, but she went as a disembodied intelligence. She didn't change anything. She entered into her own young self and guided it on exactly the same path. She set some signs or symbols, but then she let everything go on just as it had, up until she was about twelve or thirteen. At that point, she changed her past."

"Which, according to Nalavi, would have created an alternative world," she said patiently again. "Because it changed our pasts as well."

"It may have done, but only temporarily. It didn't actually change anything in Marianne's world, except as it directly affected her and her immediate family. In other words, whatever Harvey Zahmani was in Marianne's total world, it wasn't particularly important—that is, important to her, but not to the world at large. We know that because whatever alternative world may have started when he was crippled gradually converged with the old time-line and by the time Marianne reached twenty-one or -two, there was only one time-line. If we were able to look into the future of that original time-line, we would probably find that Harvey Zahmani was killed or crippled in that one as well, although perhaps at a later time. The theory of convergence would indicate that as a likelihood. Knowing Madame, it wouldn't have been much later."

"Theory of convergence," she mused. "You mean the tendency of time-lines to knit together again when they are not very far apart."

"Yes. I don't understand the logic or mathematics of it, but seemingly there is no room for an infinite number of alternative universes. They split, then converge. At any given time, only so many different ones exist. Like a river finding a new channel in flood, but still staying in the same flood plain and returning to the same channel eventually. When two people remember a specific event having happened differently, it may well be the result of a brief split and reconvergence. The event may actually have happened two ways. When a person remembers something having happened before, it may have done, on a slightly out of sync line."

"Confusing," she mused with a smile. "And terrible for you, my dear."

He sighed. "We were anchored at both ends of this particular split, so to speak, so we remember the divergence. I was never there in the years she was growing up. I only came in at the end. Nothing in what she did interrupted my time-line at all. At most I would have this tiny loop, only a few days long."

"Wasn't your *Marianne* anchored at both ends?"

"If she'd chosen to go on, yes. But she didn't." He pounded

his fist on the window sill, almost shouting. "She went—went somewhere. She simply wiped herself out of young Marianne's life after Harvey was dealt with. This left only one Marianne, which is partly why the time-line grew together again. I have a feeling the divergence was very brief and that only a few of us are able to remember it."

"My question," Ellat said, giving him a hard look, "is whether Tabiti Delubovoska remembers it. Does she remember trying to capture *Marianne* in that previous sequence?"

He shook his head. "I don't know. I hope not. I hope all she remembers is going there for a brief visit when Marianne was twelve."

"And if she does remember? Then what?"

What indeed? Vengeance? Or simply a carrying out of the original plan, whatever that was. However he rationalized it, he could not convince himself Marianne was out of danger.

"You ought to go to the Cave of Light, Makr Avehl."

"I already have," he murmured. Though none of the Kavi attendant upon the Cave of Light had ventured to tell him what the symbols meant.

"Well?" she demanded. "What did it say?"

"It showed me a woman washing clothes," he answered. "A pack of dogs. That would be the momentary gods, I'm sure of that. It showed me a palace; a dungeon. And a map."

"You consulted the lectionary?"

"Would you like me to recite the possible symbolic meanings of a woman washing clothes? Guilt. Ritual cleanliness. Labor. Redemption. There are twenty-three meanings for that symbol alone, not counting sub-categories. Would you care to know how many there are for a map?"

"Never mind, Makr Avehl. You're saying it wasn't helpful."

"I asked the Cave if I should follow Marianne to her new home, to court her, Ellat, assuming there could be anything between us at all." He fell silent, thinking of the shadow of the woman he had seen in the girl's eyes. He sighed. "Assuming there could be anything—but I got a woman washing clothes. And a map."

"A map portends a journey."

"Which was the only hopeful meaning the session produced,

believe me. Though whether it portends a journey there or a journey returning after I am refused, no one will say." He turned a scowling face toward the morning. "I continue to be worried about her, Ellat. Damn it. Something is very wrong in this new world the old *Marianne* has created, willy-nilly, but I can't get at it!"

"You left her the bracelet?"

"Of course I did."

"If she wears it, we will know of it the minute she is in danger. That is, if she goes on wearing it. Perhaps she will even be wise enough to call for our help."

"My *Marianne* might have asked for our help, yes. She had suffered. She had suspicion. She knew the world to be chaotic. She tried to protect herself against it. This Marianne? She has not suffered. Her childhood was virtually free of trauma, and she has convinced herself that all the pain was merely imaginary. She is not suspicious. She has found the world almost entirely predictable and safe."

"Ah," said Ellat in a particular tone of voice.

He took gloomy satisfaction in knowing she was not as worried as he was.

# CHAPTER 5

MARIANNE SPENT THE first week of her new job in a delirium of independence, the second week in a slough of homesickness, the third in a somewhat reasoned approach to the near future.

She looked for an old house, but there were few on the market. She had forgotten that young cities had a paucity of old homes—at least of old homes not already remodeled or wrecked in favor of urban renewal.

She reluctantly gave up the idea of owning her own place and found a pleasant apartment within walking distance of downtown, the upper floor of an old house owned by Mr. and Mrs. Apple, Patricia and Robin. Pat and Bobby. The four large rooms were freshly painted and carpeted. Cloud-haired Mama had given Marianne a generous check to use in buying furniture. She bought Mexican rugs and chunky chairs covered in bright cottons and pictures full of swirling color and one Escher print of a fish, rising to the surface of a pond amid floating leaves and reflections of sky.

She settled into work, finding it one-fifth interesting, two-fifths routine, and two-fifths utter, implacable bureaucratic bumpf. Each helpful act had to be embalmed in forms and buried in files, until she found herself feeling apprehensive about being helpful because of the amount of sheer boredom involved in making records of it.

She met a pleasant young co-worker, went out with him, told him she would not go to bed with him, and was not asked out again. She met another pleasant young co-worker who told her that knowing her almost made him regret he was gay. She met no one else.

"So this is living my own life," she snarled at herself in the mirror, fighting with her hair, which on this morning had decided to emulate Medusa and slither everywhere but where Marianne wanted it to go. "Not exactly what I had imagined."

What had she imagined?

Meaningful work. Definitely. A certain amount of elegance. That, too. A certain amount of romance? Probably.

"What's a beautiful girl like you doing sitting home?" asked Pat Apple, who had knocked at the door while Marianne was struggling with her hair.

Marianne only flushed, finding it hard to formulate an answer. "I guess I haven't been here long enough to meet anyone, really, Pat."

"How about at the office?"

"Mostly older and married. Only a couple of young ones. One of whom is a lech and the other of whom is gay. What can I tell you?"

"There are a lot of eligible men who run around in the group Robin and I do things with. Come to a few parties with us. Maybe you'll meet someone."

Pat and Robin were at least two decades older than Marianne. She had little faith in the invitation, but considerable respect for the kindness that had prompted it.

"I'll think about it, Pat. Thanks anyhow."

"Not why I came up. This package came for you while you were at work, so I signed for it."

It was an anonymous little package without a postmark. Marianne turned it in her hands, not liking the feel of it. Deep within her something stirred, a vertiginous feeling, as though some organ had come loose from its moorings and swayed. She gulped.

"Well open it, for heaven's sake. How can you just look at it like that?"

"It might be a bomb," Marianne said with a weak, unconvincing laugh. She felt nauseated.

"You know someone who'd send you a bomb?"

"Not really, no."

"Well then?"

She opened it. The cardboard of the box seemed to leave a greasy residue on her skin. Inside was crumpled, grayish tissue paper, and wrapped in that a carving made from a dark, almost grainless wood.

"What's that supposed to be? And who sent it?"

"It looks like a demon, doesn't it?" Marianne commented, disgusted by the anonymous gift or by the vagrant sickness that had gripped her. "Some kind of goblin or troll, maybe. I don't know who sent it. There's no card and no return address."

"Well, it's a nasty-looking thing. You'll probably get a card from somebody, telling you they bought it in Borneo or Tibet or someplace." Pat lumbered up from Marianne's couch and departed, calling, "You think about coming out with Robin and me, you hear?"

Behind her, Marianne stared at the hideous carving, aware that it had been done with great artistry, for the tiny, wicked eyes seemed to stay fixed on her face no matter where she moved the carving itself. She set it on the mantel, facing the wall, wanting to throw it out but unable to do so without knowing where it had come from. She sat down, huddling around herself, protecting her core without knowing she did it.

"Not Cloud-haired Mama," she said with conviction. "Not Papa. Then who?" Some friend from college? Making some kind of obscure joke? Someone from the office here? Making some equally obscure joke? "Stay there until I find out," she directed the thing as she pulled on her jacket. Her bracelet caught on the lining and she cursed, briefly, telling herself it was silly to wear Makr Avehl's gift all the time, even though he had begged her to do so.

"It really is silly to wear that all the time," a voice said in an insinuating whisper. "You don't need it. You're not in any danger."

The large clock in the lower hall began to bang away the quarter hour. Marianne stopped her effort to unlatch the bracelet and ran for the door. If she didn't leave that moment, she'd be late for work. Behind her on the mantel the carving brooded, its face toward the wall.

While fixing her breakfast the next morning, she stumbled over a featureless chunk of wood on the kitchen floor, fist sized, obviously gnawed by something with sharp, determined teeth. It was dark, almost grainless wood. She was only then reminded of the strange carving and looked for it on the mantel. It wasn't there. She had not seen it there the night before. While she was at work, someone or—or something had moved it. She stood in her kitchen with the lump of gnawed wood in her hand and shivered, very slightly, as though she had felt an icy wind. Again there was that shift inside herself, as though something sleeping had been awakened.

On her way out she asked, "Pat, you and Robin don't have a dog, do you?"

"Robin's allergic. I used to have a cat. Why? You have mice or something?"

"No. I just . . . thought I heard a dog, that's all."

The day at work did not go well. The computer files on artificial insemination and experimental breeding programs, which she had spent the past three weeks building, were now fatally corrupted, and she screamed silently at the thought of rebuilding them. Everyone who called seemed to need information from the corrupted files.

"How did this happen?" she demanded from the world at large.

"Software," the hardware consultant opined.

"Hardware," the software support person snarled.

Neither of them was helpful. In her mind a demon face watched her from tiny eyes, and she found herself remembering the carving that had been on her mantel.

She had driven to work that morning in order to use the car for shopping after work. When she went to the parking lot, she had a flat tire.

On the way home, late and weary, a scant twenty blocks, she

narrowly escaped an accident when two cars in front of her collided.

In her apartment, the chewed chunk of wood had found its way back to her mantel. She laid wood in the fireplace and set it ablaze, waiting until a crackling fire was going before tossing the featureless chunk of wood on top. It hissed agonizingly, finally exploding in a shower of glowing coals. The firescreen caught them, harmlessly. There was an odor of sulphur. She shivered, something she could not quite remember teasing at the edges of her mind.

In the morning, she went to her office in a fatalistic mood, prepared to spend all of the next few weeks restoring the ruined files. She was greeted with smiles from the software support woman. "Good news. You've got your files back. I got into the system last night and got around the glitch, whatever it was."

The morning went by in a flurry of productive, interesting work. Just after lunch, the phone rang and Pat Apple said, "A package came for you, Marianne. I signed for it and put it up in your apartment. Hope that's OK?"

She assured Pat it was okay, then turned to the restored files. They had disappeared again. Only gibberish came up on her screen.

She sat very still for five minutes, then left the office and walked home. She did not really believe there was any connection, and yet—the two events had followed very closely. A hex, perhaps? If there were any such thing. She laughed at herself unconvincingly.

In her living room she found the remnants of a cardboard box, scraps of grayish tissue paper, a faintly musty smell. On the carpet lay fragments of grainless wood, obviously chewed.

She built a fire and put all the remnants on the flames. When they started to burn, she heard her own voice saying, "All right. Which one of you is it?"

From behind the curtains came the Dingo Dog, yellow eyes gleaming at her. She sat, head turned a little, regarding Marianne out of the corner of her eyes. Marianne caught her breath, a deep, choking gasp, as though she could not get enough air in her lungs to speak. She had thought all the old hallucinations and visions were behind her. She was grown-up now. Real was what real was. She wanted no more of this fantasy, and yet here were her childhood visions, come to life again. Her voice asked, "Did you chew it up because it was dangerous? Is that why?" It was her voice, and yet she had not asked the question.

The Dingo whined. She remembered then that the Dingo had never spoken, not like the others.

"Are the rest of you around, too?"

"From time to time," said a breathy voice in a peculiar accent. "From time to time." The Red Foo Dog came from the bathroom, jauntily. Just behind it the Dragon Dog came slithering, crawling on its belly, as though begging to be petted. Her bedroom door creaked open. She could see the Wolf Bitch lying on her bed, her huge head pillowed on her crossed paws. Beside her lay the Black Dog, asleep, eyes shut and red mouth agape.

"Why?"

"Bad thing, that was," the Dragon Dog said. "That thing you got in the boxes. Very bad creature, that one, as us creatures go. Had to chew it up, get it to go away."

"You have to burn them," the foreign, not-herself voice said, "or you'll not get rid of them." In the fireplace the thing she had tried to burn had turned into something quite horrible that screamed as it incinerated. So, she was dreaming. There was no need for rejection of what was going on around her. She would merely play along, waiting until she woke up.

"Fire isn't one of our things," the Foo Dog said. "We have others, but not fire."

"Someone's after you," the Wolf said from the bedroom. "Someone very nasty."

"Have you been here all along?" she asked, ignoring what the Wolf had said. She didn't want to hear it.

"Off and on," said the Black Dog. "When we had time."

"I thought maybe . . . maybe'd you'd gone back to—to wherever *Marianne* got you from."

"She got us from our own loci," the Foo Dog said. "Every locus in the universe has one of us attendant to it. We give material space its reality by giving time its duration. Each moment is dependent upon us. Hence, momentary gods."

"But if you're not in your proper—locus, then what happens to the universe?" she asked, trying to keep her mind off the mess in the fireplace that had stopped screaming and started hissing as it boiled away to nothing.

"We're there," said the Foo Dog. "And here. Being in two places at once is very common for a momentary god. We're basically a wave form with particular aspects."

"Someone asked me if I had dismissed you," she said, trying to remember who.

"We were very gratified when you did not," the Wolf Bitch said, licking her nose. "Being away from one's nexus is stimulating."

In the fireplace, the thing subsided with a final whimper into a pile of ash. Marianne looked at it. She was not sure what it had been. She did not want to see it again.

"What do you think that was?" she asked, pointing.

"It could have been one of us," the Foo Dog said, turning to the Dragon Dog. "Do you think it was one of us momegs? I thought for a moment it looked rather familiar. When it started to yell."

Dragon Dog nodded, "One of us. Whoever summoned it had built a dismissal in, however. When you burned it, Marianne, you dismissed it. It went back, wherever it belonged."

"But it wasn't shaped like a dog. I thought maybe all momentary gods . . ."

The Black Dog rolled over and laughed at her out of blood-red eyes. "Momegs for short, Marianne. Why should it have resembled a dog? Among the infinite loci in the universe you will find an infinity of gods, momegs, one of every conceivable shape and kind and power, no two alike, though many may be similar. We five are merely similar. We are not alike. That we are doglike is not coincidental. *Marianne* picked us for that reason. She needed doglike creatures for what you—she—meant to do."

"It wasn't me, but pass that for the moment. How did I—she—know where you were?"

"If you don't know that, how do you expect us to know? Somehow you knew. She knew. You summoned us."

"But I—she—didn't dismiss you?"

"For which we are grateful. Our gratitude explains why we have taken the trouble to remain close at hand, to provide such guardianship as possible."

"I didn't do it because I didn't know how," she confessed, thinking even as she did so that it might be dangerous to be that honest about her own ignorance. "I wish you'd realize it wasn't me. It really wasn't!"

"What was she is now you," the Foo Dog said, not unkindly. "We can only address her by addressing you. She gave herself for you. You don't seem grateful."

"If you thought about it, you'd know how I feel," she snapped. Even knowing it was a dream didn't protect her from anger. "How would you like it if someone you didn't know laid some great burden on you before you were born. So, she stopped being. I'm sorry. I go on being. I'm not sorry about that. She didn't dismiss you, maybe because she forgot or didn't know how, any more than I do. What are we talking about it for?"

*"Let me wake up,"* she thought. *"Please, let this go on by and I'll wake up."*

The Foo Dog commented, "You didn't know how, true. But you took no steps to learn how to dismiss us, either. That means you didn't mind our being loose. For which we are, as we have said, grateful. Our gratitude must now take some palpable and practical form toward whichever of you is available to us. We must offer such advice and help as we can. It must be obvious even to you, Marianne, that you are under attack."

She shook her head, not willing to concede this.

"Oh yes. Yesterday's mishaps were not a mere run of ill luck. Other misfortunes undoubtedly began today the minute that crystalized momeg arrived in your space, your 'turf,' so to speak. Just as each momeg has its own locus, its own point in space, and it's own nexus, that is its continuum, so each living thing has a 'turf,' a set of material concatenations arranged in a highly personal and largely inflexible way. When an outside momeg intrudes—so to speak—without invitation, the turf is warped. Visualize it as a tray of tightly packed marbles into which one more is pushed, one that doesn't fit. . . ." The Foo Dog lifted her hind leg and chewed a rear paw, reflectively.

"Chaos often results."

Marianne nodded, unable to speak. This dream had to end soon. What was she doing, sitting here on her apartment floor, talking to five dogs, four of whom talked back.

The Dingo whined and put a paw on her leg.

"Dingo wants you to know she is no less concerned than the rest of us, Marianne. After all, there is one built-in form of dismissal with all momegs. When the summoner dies, the momeg dismisses. Just like that. If we wish to stay free, we will continue to be concerned with your welfare."

"This is nonsense. Who would attack me, and why?"

Black Dog jumped down from the bed and strolled to the front window where he sat, ruby eyes staring out at the afternoon. Foo Dog went to the dining-room window. Wolf Dog sat up and glared out of the bedroom window. Dingo padded her way into the bathroom and Marianne heard her nails scratching the sill. Dragon Dog merely sat where he was. Dingo whined as she came back into the room. The others reassembled, nodding their furry heads.

"Someone's watching you, Marianne," said the Foo Dog. "Not from nearby. From some distance away, but watching you, nonetheless."

"A woman?" she asked, dreading the answer. "Is it a woman?" She was remembering what Makr Avehl had said, his warnings that she had dismissed.

"I smelled a woman," Dragon Dog said. "Unmistakably."

Dingo whined in disagreement.

"No, I grant you it didn't look like a woman, but nonetheless that's what I smelled." Dragon Dog sniffed. "Dingo says the person watching you looks like a cloud of darkness with eyes."

"Tall," she said, half hysterically, trying to remember what Madame Delubovoska had looked like in that long-ago childhood time. "Very thin. With black, black hair and brows."

"She smells like black hair, yes. Thin, with very black hair and a bad disposition."

Dingo whined again.

"Well, that's what I said, wasn't it?" Dragon Dog growled. "Dingo insists on 'evil disposition' rather than merely bad."

"There's only one person it could be. Madame Delubovoska. My half brother's aunt." Shaken out of her tenuous composure, lost in a seeming reality of danger, Marianne ran to the phone and punched long distance, jittering from foot to foot as she waited for an answer, telling herself she was not really calling, that it was only a dream call for which she would never receive a bill. . . .

"Mama? How are you? How's Papa?"

"Oh, yes, I miss everyone. And everything. Listen, are you all right? Is everyone there OK? No, nothing's wrong. I just got homesick, I guess."

In the quiet apartment, the five momentary gods scratched, sniffed, groomed themselves, and nibbled at itchy places while Marianne concluded her conversation. "Madame hasn't done anything to them," she said at last. "Not to Mama, or Papa. Last time—that other time, didn't she do something to them, first?"

"This is a new time," said the Black Dog in his great, baying voice. "This is a new time. And in this time, you may wish to put an end to the danger once and for all, Marianne. When you decide what you want to do . . . call on us."

He turned and walked into the wallpaper. When she turned, the others were gone, Dingo's tail just disappearing into a kitchen cabinet.

When she decided what she wanted to do?

What could she do?

She raised her hand to her forehead, rubbing it, the pendant crystal that Makr Avehl had given her twinkling in the light from her west window. When she woke up, she would really call home.

She lay down on the couch, shutting her eyes. It was only a vision. Overwork. Homesickness. Stress. Reversion to an infantile fantasy life. She breathed deeply, willing herself to go into deep, unconscious sleep. She would wake, and it would be gone—all of it. Only a dreamed up nonsense put together from fairy tales and recollections. The dogs were only her memory of the dogs that had attacked Harvey. The dark woman was only a remake of Disney's Snow White with its evil, hollow-cheeked queen. "Mirror, mirror on the wall," she chanted to herself defiantly.

Black Dog stuck his head out of the mirror and said in a stern voice, "Mockery does not become you, Marianne."

She turned over on the sofa pillow and wept herself truly asleep.

# CHAPTER 6

WHEN SHE AWOKE in the morning, she tried to convince herself it had all been hallucination, brought about by stress, incited by the unpleasant gifts that someone had sent her. Staring at her own face in the mirror, she was unable to decide whether she really believed this or not. Before she went to work, she asked Pat Apple not to accept any more mail that had to be signed for. "I don't care what it is, Pat. Letter, package, leaflet, registered mail—just don't sign for it. Let them leave me a notice and I'll pick it up. That box you signed for was a nasty joke, and it exploded when I opened it. . . ."

"Exploded!" Pat screamed. "My god, Marianne . . ."

"No damage done. It was all a joke. But it made a rotten smell, and I don't want any more. So, Okay?"

"If I had friends who did things like that, they'd get a piece of my mind," Pat grumbled. "Honestly. Do I need to fumigate up there or anything? Deodorize?"

"It's all right now. Just don't accept anything else."

She left feeling both prudent and dissatisfied, as though there were something else she should have done but could not remember. Some precaution in addition to the one she had just taken. What had this vague threat amounted to after all?

Someone had played a couple of nasty jokes on her that had evoked her childhood fantasies, that's all. Nothing of any moment. Nothing she wasn't able to deal with—mostly by ignoring it.

And yet, perhaps there was something else she should have done. Something. On her wrist, the crystal bracelet sparkled in the morning light, unregarded. She was too preoccupied to notice it.

The day passed without incident. Friday followed, placid as a summer meadow. The weekend came and went. She did her laundry, went to a movie, told herself she had gotten over it, whatever it had been.

Monday, when she came home from work, there were chalk marks on the walk, looping swirls of yellow and red chalk, vertiginous spirals extending from the gate to the porch. Something inside her lurched, as though some essential organ had turned over, realigning itself into an unaccustomed position. Marianne gritted her teeth and crossed the lines, stepping from space to space in the design as though the marks had been barriers, surprised to find herself doing it without thought, more surprised to feel the wave of sheer terror that washed over her and was as unaccountably gone in the instant.

Pat was on the porch. "Who's been messing up the sidewalk?" Marianne asked, looking back at the writhing lines, wondering what had just happened.

"Kids playing hopscotch, I suppose," Pat said vaguely, fanning herself with a magazine. "Doesn't really look like the hopscotch I remember, but things change. The marks were there about noon when I went out to get the mail. Funny. I did just what you did, walked in the spaces. A holdover from childhood, don't you suppose? It's been so hot today, I've been falling asleep all afternoon.

Pat still looked half asleep, as though drugged, and her enervation seemed to be catching. It was like yawning, Marianne thought, opening her eyes wide and shaking her head. You see someone yawn, and it makes you yawn. She felt the same energy-draining lassitude Pat seemed to be feeling. It had not been this hot earlier; almost tropical. And wet. The stairs were an endless climb, as though to some precipice.

There were more curiously twisted chalk marks on the upstairs hall floor and one on her apartment door. Some children must have come into the hallway and played around—Pat Apple often left the entry door unlocked. Marianne did not have the energy to rub the design out. Her key turned effortlessly.

The door opened.

Her eyes on the chalk marks, she went through . . .

In Alphenlicht, Makr Avehl sat up in bed, a shout trembling on his lips. There had been a flash, a very vivid flash. Someone knocked on his door.

"Come in, Ellat."

"Something's happened to her, Makr Avehl."

"I know. I felt it."

"What are we going to do?"

"I don't know. I'm going to try to reach her. . . ."

"She won't be there."

"You think not?" He belted a robe around himself, rubbing his face with both hands.

"I know not. The crystal wouldn't have flashed if she were still there. She's been moved. Like last time."

"Not quite. No. I don't think she consented verbally this time. It's some other variety of Madame's doing. Something more subtle. Oh, by the Gods and the Cave, I really didn't expect anything this soon. . . ."

"Makr Avehl."

"Yes, Ellat."

"Maybe you shouldn't go after her. Maybe it's meant to end as it ended. She isn't the woman you loved. You admit that."

He stared at his feet, wondering how he was to tell her, how he was to convince himself. "Maybe she isn't the woman I loved, Ellat. But the woman I loved is still there."

"Makr Avehl!"

"It's true. I'd stake my soul on it. She's there. Buried. Unconscious. No. She's sleeping, Ellat. Sleeping and dreaming. Peering out at the world from time to time with wide, blinded, forsaken eyes."

"You saw?"

"I saw what I thought was my *Marianne*. For an instant, only. Inside this other woman, somewhere."

"Why? How?"

"I think she made a trade. Her life for Harvey's. She couldn't kill herself, so she just stopped . . . stopped being. No. Stopped expressing her being. She still *is*, but she doesn't give her existence any expression at all. She's just asleep." He sighed deeply, feeling the familiar anguish that he had felt only weeks before when his *Marianne* had vanished, as suddenly, as cruelly.

"And even if that weren't true, even if Marianne is not the woman I loved at all, still she is in this difficulty at least partly because of what I did or didn't do. In a sense, this is my responsibility."

"So you're going to go after her anyhow, aren't you?"

He didn't answer. The expression on his face was answer enough.


. . . through the door into her living room. It had a tidal smell to it, an abiding moisture, as though the sweats and steams from the laundry below had permeated the intervening walls and floor, making a swamp of these few rooms. Each evening when she climbed the narrow, dank stairs and opened the splintery door she expected to see crabs scurrying away behind the couch or a stand of cattails waving in the kitchen door. She would not have been amazed to find fish swimming in the kitchen sink or leaping in the tub. The greenish undersea colors of the worn carpet and the walls did nothing to refute this expectation. She was always surprised when she did not float into the place rather than plodding, as now, like an unwilling diver, across the sea floor of living room into a watery cave of kitchen to put the kettle on.

Most of her furniture had been collected from among things left in the laundry over the years. The bed had been found in the big indigo washer one evening after locking up. The green armchair had turned up in a dryer early one morning, though she thought she had checked the machine the night before as she had been told to do. Dishes and cushions appeared frequently, sometimes in the rose machine and sometimes in the green one.

Once she had found a roaster and three live chickens in the ivory dryer. She had put the roaster on a high shelf in the kitchen; the three chickens still scratched a meagre living out of the weedy yard behind the laundry, nesting hopefully along the dilapidated board fence. One of them was, or believed itself to be, a rooster and greeted each day with a throaty chuckle that both it and Marianne supposed to be a crow. The cry had more of apologetics than of evangelism about it. On hearing it each morning, Marianne murmured "pardon me," as though she had been guilty of some egregious incongruity in harboring such an unsuitable chanticleer.

In addition to the more or less salvageable things found in the machines, there were great quantities of miscellany that she could find no use for. These she hauled out, as best she could, into the rear yard near the alley gate, and the trash men picked them up once each week or, for a sizeable tip, fetched the detritus from the laundry itself. She was always afraid that the tips, though accounted for on petty-cash slips and meticulously itemized, would not be considered acceptable expenses and would be deducted from her already tiny paycheck. Surely they could not expect her—or any one person—to carry the quantities of heavy things that the machines disgorged. Why, only two days ago there had been three sets of elephant harness as well as a crated harmonium and three pictures of the palace!

She had hung the pictures among the others in her office. Pictures of the palace or of the royal family almost covered the office walls, repetitive arrangements of the perpendicular: tall, thin members of the ruling family echoing tall, thin columns of the east portico, further paralleled by tall, thin trees on either side. Marianne could not remember seeing the palace personally, though the laundry must surely have been close to it at some time in the past. Still, she kept the pictures. It seemed less disrespectful than throwing them away. Disrespect was punishable, and she supposed she would start hanging them in the laundry itself when the walls of her office were filled.

The office was a mere cubicle in the rear corner of the laundry, a flimsy box of wallboard with one glass window set into it through which she could watch the customers at the machines and two doors, one leading to the back stairway and one into the laundry itself. That one she could shut when the noise became too overpowering, the sound of surf and whirlpool and tide and storm, a rush and surge and shush-shush of waters, a hum and whirl of air.

As one entered from the usually cobbled street one saw the seven huge machines down the left-hand wall, each labeled as to suggested contents, facing the seven matching dryers on the right-hand wall. Ivory washer opposite ivory dryer. Rose machine opposite rose machine. Great, indigo mechanism looming opposite another, equally monstrous. And on the back wall, the small, specialized machines, palest pink and baby blue and sea green, with their tiny soap dispensers tidily arrayed nearby.

In the center of the room was the spotting table and the table for folding clean laundry and half a dozen hard, molded chairs, reliably uncomfortable. The place was busy enough. No point in encouraging people to sit about by making it inviting.

She put the cash box on the kitchen table with a sense of relief, feeling more tired than usual tonight. It had been a sins day, with half the population of Badigor seeking redemption, and Marianne hadn't had time to sit down since seven this morning. The indigo washer had jammed along about noon, losing at least a dozen citizens in the process. They might show up again, or they might not. With Marianne's luck, she thought dismally, they'd show up in one of the dryers in the middle of the night and wake her up with their pounding and gargled cries for release.

The apartment looked strange to her, too, as it did sometimes. As though she hadn't really seen it before, wasn't familiar with it, didn't belong in it. As though when she opened the door she should have been somewhere else. Somewhere drier, she thought, closing her eyes and visualizing it. A place where things didn't rust or mildew immediately. A place with a fireplace and light coming in through the windows instead of this constant, deadly fog. The thought of the fog made her think of being lost, and this brought her alert in a sudden panic.

She hadn't bought her map for tomorrow!

She stood up, mouth open in an expression of unconscious anxiety, hands twisting together. Usually she bought the map at noon, at a news vendor's kiosk. There was always a news vendor's kiosk somewhere within three or four blocks. Today she hadn't had time to go out to lunch, and she had forgotten it until this moment.

She fought panic by checking her watch, noting that she had at least fifteen minutes before the kiosk would close for the night. If she didn't get the map there, the nearest place would be the all-night restaurant at the corner of—there, she'd forgotten already. She'd need today's map in order to find either location.

She grabbed up the map and peered at it as she ran down the stairs, down the aisle between the monstrous, silent machines, their doors agape like snoring mouths, and out the door, stopping under the street light to find the nearest kiosk. There was one, just three blocks away!

She hurried, half running, paying little attention to her surroundings. At one time, she seemed to recall, she had spent hours just walking, entertaining herself with speculation about the strange houses and buildings and with the odd juxtapositions she discovered—infant nursery beside slaughterhouse; twin brothels flanking a church; doctors and apothecaries adjacent to mortuaries; a manufacturer of ear plugs next to a teacher of music. She seemed to remember that she had laughed at these arrangements once, with genuine amusement. No longer. She could not imagine what had made her think them laughable. Humor resulted from surprise, and the combinations she had found were not novel, not even unusual. If she had found them funny, it meant there was something wrong with her, something different, something that didn't fit in. It was almost as though she had come from some other world in which such neighbors were unlikely. This idea had popped into her head unbidden, frightening her badly. The Map Police were known to seek out strangers, people who didn't fit in. She did not wish to be sought out, so she had stopped looking for weird combinations, stopped noticing the buildings she passed except for ones marking her progress toward her infrequent destinations. It was better just to stick to one's own obligatory business: a trip to a kiosk once a day to buy a map, a trip to take the laundry receipts to a bank and to shop at a grocery once every ten days, a trip to whatever temple or shrine was nearby on the infrequently declared holidays.

People who used the laundry sometimes talked of keeping in touch with friends or relatives. On holidays, they would meet in a previously agreed upon park. Or they would select a certain restaurant and gather there.

"I wanted to celebrate Mother's birthday," one woman had said plaintively over her crocheting. "But how would anyone know when it was?"

Marianne found herself wondering what a birthday was. Some kind of holiday she didn't know about. She, herself, had never known anyone well enough to meet them on a holiday. Whenever a holiday was announced, she would make her obligatory trip to the temple or shrine or church and then come back to the apartment over the laundry. She had no relatives. At least, she supposed she had none. Surely she would know if she had, she thought, hurrying along the empty street. It was the kind of thing a person ought to know.

The kiosk was in the middle of the block. The vendor had his back to her and was lowering the shutter as she approached. "Tomorrow's map, please," she called, her voice bouncing shrilly between buildings, a dwindling flutter of retreating sound. "I'm sorry I'm so late."

"So late is too late," he grumbled, turning his lumpy face toward her, the eroded skin circling a red, pendulous nose that swayed slightly as he turned. "All sold out."

"Oh, no!" she cried. "You can't be."

"Can't, can't I? Oh, yes I can. I say out, I mean I haven't got any. Except one for me. Now, if you'd like to share it?" He leaned toward her, one hand out as though to touch her, his face twisted into a suggestive leer. She turned away, keeping her face quiet, trying to be dignified about it. No doubt he meant what he said; he'd share if she'd come home with him, and it would be legal to do so. Cohabitors could share maps. Mothers and children. Married couples. Lovers. She shuddered in revulsion at the idea of sharing anything with the vendor who stood watching her, his nose twitching. Before he could say anything more, she moved away, fumbling with the map, which resisted being unfolded, almost as though it were a living thing with a natural resentment at being disturbed.

She had circled the laundry with red pencil, almost at the

edge of the map, far from its important, stable center. From there she traced her way to the kiosk where she was now, then searched for the nearest location marked with a spoon and a large, red "24." There were two twenty-four-hour restaurants within reasonable traveling distance. The street she was on ran directly toward one of them, then circled away at a narrow alley labeled "Mock Street." If she could catch a number twenty-seven bus—the number clearly marked on the map—and get off at Mock Street, it would be a walk of only a few blocks.

She went directly to the bus stop, ignoring whatever it was the vendor shouted after her, checking carefully to be sure the number twenty-seven stopped at this particular place. It was a favorite trick of the mappers to have busses halt at only every third or fourth stop, letting the people in between stand helplessly as the bus rumbled by, clattering over cobbles or sections of trolley track that led nowhere but seemed always to crop up in three or four block-long sections. This stop was scheduled for number twenty-seven busses at twenty-minute intervals.

What was scheduled had no connection with what actually happened. No bus arrived. She jittered, moving to and fro on the pavement. There was a vengeance booth on the corner, and the vendor leaned from behind her counter to solicit Marianne's business. "Fine, fresh vengeance fish," she called. "Caught just this morning and spell cast before it was dead. Name it for your enemy and let him eat it. Stop his heart, stop his mind, stop his life, lady?"

"I don't have any enemies," Marianne called softly. "I don't need a fish, thank you."

"No enemies? Think of that. Here in this city, and she says she has no enemies?" The woman cackled with laughter and closed the booth front. When Marianne looked up a moment later, she had gone, and Marianne sighed with relief. Sometimes the vendors were very persistent. Twice or three times, she had bought things that she didn't want, carried them home with her, and then had to put them out for the trash men. There had been a set of thumb screws, she remembered. And a whip braided out of human hair with little sharp bones set in it. Things that made her squirm with revulsion when she looked at them. She sighed, turning to stare down the street in the direction the bus should come from.

When forty-five minutes had passed, however, none had arrived. She counseled herself sternly not to start walking. As soon as she did, particularly if she were in between widely separated stops, the bus would come and pass her by. She checked her watch. Eight o'clock. Plenty of time. It was only a half-hour ride, and the streets would not shift until midnight. Eleven at the earliest. Or ten-thirty. Plenty of time.

She shifted from foot to foot, staring down the street, uttering silent invocations. "Bus, good bus, come on, bus."

At eight-thirty, she began to worry. If she started now, she could reach the all-night restaurant by walking. If she waited too long, it would be impossible to reach it at all. Good sense warred with her weariness. She didn't want to make the long walk.

"You have to," she told herself. "You have to."

She turned and strode down the street, checking her progress against the map at every crossing. It would be a walk of some sixty blocks. About five miles. She could be there well before shift time.

A number twenty-seven bus passed her by and stopped two blocks down the street. She began to run, senselessly, knowing it wouldn't wait.

It pulled out just as she came close enough to touch the rear of it. A man who was passing shook his head and murmured, "Tough luck. Why don't you just wait for the next one?"

She checked her watch. Nine o'clock. There wasn't time to wait. She lowered her head and kept walking. Another twenty-seven bus went by. She let it go. She had a hard, burning pain in her side and could not possibly run again. The pain in her side moved downward, slowly, first into her hip and then into her right knee and shin. The door of the orange dryer had fallen open and bruised her there. The half-healed muscle still hurt, more and more the farther she walked.

There were infrequent passersby. Sometimes people looked each other full in the face, as though searching for a face they knew. Other times, they ducked their heads and scurried past, as though afraid to encounter either an acquaintance or a stranger. Marianne, on her infrequent forays from the laundry, tried to take her cue from those she passed, but tonight she was too tired to care. She stared at her feet as people went by, praying they would not say anything to delay her.

By ten o'clock she had reached Mock Street. The all-night restaurant was now only a dozen blocks away, but the street she was on turned into a massive concrete overpass, soaring above the surrounding area. The next street over dived down, as though into a tunnel, and did not emerge again for blocks. There were half a dozen access ramps circling up and over, down and under, allowing access to every street except the one she needed. She puzzled at them, plotting her route. If she went down Mock Street one block then turned left she would come to an underpass that would take her under a highway and bring her within two blocks of the restaurant.

She trudged on. The street lights in this part of town threw puddles of dim, dun-yellow light onto the pavement and reflected a furtive glow into alleys and along the curbs, hiding as much as it disclosed. She stopped momentarily, thinking what might be hiding in those alleys. There were stories about bears living in alleys and crocodiles in the sewers under the street. And there were mapless gangs, not storied but real, ever-changing tribes of non-locus aberrants who preyed upon single pedestrians.

The underpass before her was not lighted at all except by a grayish shine at the far end, a perfect location for ambush. She dithered, trying to see if anything lurked against the distant glow, plunging into the semi-darkness at last in an almost fatalistic fit of panic. She got to the center of it, the deepest part, buffeted to the far edge of the sidewalk by gusts kicked up by passing trucks, when there was a shudder, a gelatinous shiver.

"No," she said. "No." It had only been the vibration of the heavy trucks, she told herself. It couldn't have been the changeover. It was far too early.

The tunnel seemed endless. When she emerged, the street sign nearest her said "Willis Boulevard." She turned to her map, only to see it shrivel in her hands and fall to the sidewalk in bits of ash, twisting in the light wind, disappearing around an anonymous corner. She stood at an intersection with featureless walls looming around her. A loudspeaker on the lamppost bellowed white noise at her, then muttered, "Welcome to the City of Trallis."

"Oh, God, no," she moaned. "God, please, no."

The map she had used was obsolete. There was no more Badigor. She was too late. Now she could not buy a map that would tell her where anything was today. It was illegal—perhaps impossible—to sell anyone a map of today. Only tomorrow's maps would be available. It was illegal—or impossible—for anyone to share a map with her. She would be unable to find anything except by chance. And if she did not chance upon a map vendor, then the day after today would be even further lost.

She had had nightmares about this, as she imagined most of the people of the city did, though many would not admit doing so. She had considered what she would do if ever she found herself without a map. The one thing she had resolved upon was that she would kill herself before she would join the mapless ones with her name tattooed on her face and her hair dyed green.

"Search," she told herself. "I've got to search."

"Sleep," some interior voice demanded. "You've got to sleep, first."

She couldn't sleep on the street. She had money in her money belt, plus what was in her wallet. Only idiots went anywhere without money. She could find somewhere to sleep. Perhaps a hotel.

Something.

She began to walk. There were few signs on the buildings, and it would not have mattered if there were more or fewer. Juxtaposition meant nothing. The large blue building with the carved cornerstone—"Wilkins Building, July 16, 1917"—might have stood next to the red stone building yesterday, as it did today, or it might have stood halfway across the district. Only the map and the directory could have told her. If one knew the name of the building, one could look it up in the directory, find the coordinates on the map, then find the building itself. If one didn't know the name of the building or have a map—then one was lost.

"Lost," she whispered to herself. "Lord, I'm lost."

This block was lined with four- and five-story, narrow fronted apartment houses with ornate, Italianate cornices. From high above her the sound of a radio whined into darkness and a white curtain flapped from a dark window, a ghost making a futile attempt at escape. At the end of the block she turned one block left along a muddy path beside a dairy farm, then resumed her original direction. This was a warehouse area, lined with featureless walls and locked entries fronted with iron grates. Sometimes glassy doors showed a light from some back room filtering through to the street in a pallid, fungoid glow.

She moved left another block, a boardwalk past two gambling houses, then onto a tesselated pavement outside the townhouse of some grandee. At the corner, a neon sign identified a drugstore. She went in, searching fruitlessly for the symbol that would have identified the place as a map vendor. None. There was hot coffee, however, and a sweet, sticky doughnut, sustenance for the search. She went out again, noting in passing that she stood at the corner of Bruce and RP4. She walked down Bruce, crossing Eleanor and 5V and Shimstacks. Halfway down the block she entered a place that looked slightly like a hotel but turned out to be a brothel. Redfaced, she returned to the street.

"Quittin' early, sweetheart?" asked a constable, burly in his codpiece and high-laced sandals. He was loud enough to attract the attention of passersby.

"I thought it was a hotel," she said without thinking.

"No map, eh? Move it, girly. No loitering." He stood looking after her, slapping his riot gun into one beefy palm, a sneer on his face that she could feel through her light jacket. "You should've applied for a job," he yelled after her as she turned the corner. "Then you'd know where you are!" Through the furious pounding of her blood in her ears, she could hear his laughter halfway down the next block, joined by that of the sycophants on the street corner.

Police persecuted non-locus people as legitimate prey. They harrassed people whose eyes were bad, as well, people who had trouble reading the maps. Or even foreigners who had trouble with the language. So far as the police were concerned, ignorance of the map was no excuse. She trudged on, leaving the dirty laughter behind.

She no longer tried to make an orderly search pattern. In order to avoid making circles, she turned alternately right and left, without any particular system. When she was so tired she could scarcely drag one foot in front of another, the street lights went off and she found herself in front of an all-night diner. She stared at the door for long, unconscious minutes before recognizing the red "24" painted on the glass. A map vendor.

She ordered coffee, went into the rest room and took enough money from her belt to pay for tomorrow's map, cursing in futile anger when she caught the crystal in her bracelet on the belt and could not get loose for long moments. "Get rid of that bracelet," she told herself in an unfamiliar voice. "It's always catching on things." As she was about to unclasp it and throw it away, however, someone came into the rest room and distracted her. Getting tomorrow's map was the important thing, she reminded herself. It would not help her today, but at the next shift, she would be able to find her way home.

"Gettin' it early, eh," the counterman said as he handed her the map. "Always smart to have your map early. Glad to see you, too. Didn't think I'd have any business today. Hate it when I end up surrounded by warehouses this way. At least, I guess they're warehouses. Just bad for business."

"I suppose it would be better in the theatre district," Marianne remarked. "People staying out late."

He nodded judiciously. "That's a nice idea, a theatre district. Don't know I've ever seen a theatre district, if you mean a place where the theatres sort of cluster. Not much clustering any more. Lately it seems like every shift scatters things out more and more. I was surprised to see all these warehouses near each other this way when I came down to work this morning, to tell you the truth. Where I was yesterday, there was an aristocrat's mansion on one side of me and a junkyard on the other, and down the side streets was an amusement park and three office buildings. The noble had his screen up all day. Didn't blame him, either. That roller coaster practically ended up in my back booth."

Marianne said something innocuous and noncommital.

"You on your way to work?"

She nodded, putting down coins to pay for the coffee, saying thank you, going out the door into the light of day with no idea where she was.

No one would be there to open the laundry. It might be all right. Business would be light on the day after sin day. Her legs felt like lead weights. She could not possibly lift them to walk another step. She had to find someplace she could sit, someplace she could stay until the next shift. A movie theatre. A park. No one would bother her in either place. . . .

She walked slowly, pausing frequently to rest, leaning against fences, perching briefly on window sills while she pretended to take nonexistent stones out of her shoes. Shadows moved from one side of things to the other. She came to a botanical garden, which made her think of benches. After a moment's consideration, she paid the small fee to enter and moved among the scanty viewers along the sandy walks.

There was a grove of snatch trees set behind high fences with warning posters every few feet. Just past the snatch trees, a shallow lagoon was bordered with wide-mouthed maneaters, the ground littered with bones and the air thick with attractant scent. A weary-looking woman leaned pensively upon the protective wall, watching silently as the two oldest of her five screaming children teetered atop it. When they dropped safely to the ground beside her, she sighed, smiled apologetically at Marianne, and moved away toward the panther bushes where the barricades were in worse repair.

Beyond the homovores was a vegetable exhibition; beyond that a formal garden and reflecting pool; and beyond that an Oriental garden with a curved bridge over a chuckling stream and a miniature teahouse perched high upon a rock. People turned and moved curiously toward sounds of tragedy from the vicinity of the panther bushes. In moments Marianne was alone. The teahouse seemed to smile down at her from its perch. Without thought, she stepped across the bridge, climbed through the shrubbery and into the little structure, like a child into her own dollhouse. It was only six feet across. She lay down, stretched along one wall, hidden from any passerby. Immediately, she slept, curled like a cat, shivering, but oblivious to the outside world.

When she woke, it was almost dusk. She could not remember

where she was. She should have been in her apartment. "Pat," she said. "This room is ridiculously small for the rent I pay." The words left no echo. They were forgotten as she spoke them. When she struggled out of the tiny house and across the bridge once more, the gates around the Oriental garden were closed and locked, six feet of close chain link with barbed wire at the top, both fence and wire red with rust but quite sound, for all that. She cried soundlessly as she walked back to the bridge, returning there because it would give her a sense of familiarity, however spurious. She sat for a time on the teahouse steps, watching the shadows grow thick among the carefully trimmed evergreens, listening to the lilt of water under the curved bridges. There was a boar scarer in the pool, a length of bamboo that filled with water, became overbalanced to spill the water out, then tipped back to let its momentarily empty length fall with an echoing blow onto a river-rounded stone. She had not noticed the sound in the afternoon among the chatter of sightseers and the cries of children. Now it seemed a drumbeat, slightly too slow to anticipate, coming each time as a surprise, like a hostile blow or shout.

She wept angrily. What good did it do to have tomorrow's map if one was locked up . . . though the gates would be unlocked fairly early in the morning. Perhaps. One couldn't be sure of that. Tomorrow might be declared a holiday, and nothing would be unlocked.

"Stop this," she told herself. "Don't just sit here. Find a way out!"

She began to wander, aimlessly, down across the high-backed bridges, toward the back of the garden where a fence of bamboo stood behind low evergreens and flowering shrubs. There was an unlocked gate. Behind it, she found a shed with loose boards making up the back wall of the gardens. She slipped through into a trash-filled yard only half a block from an evening world of restaurants and theatres.

She was sitting in one of the restaurants, finishing a third cup of coffee when the shift came. It was a soundless vibration, as though the world had been made of gelatine and was shaken, very slightly, making the outlines of everything quiver in semi-liquid confusion. All around her, silence fell, people looked at one another from the corners of their eyes, waiting for any sign that someone in the room might be non-locus. "Welcome," blared the loudspeakers, "to the City of Bimbarn-legume." Waiters began brushing up the scattered fragments of yesterday's maps; conversation resumed, people fished out their maps of today, plotting their way home or to whatever late evening diversion they had planned. The restaurant was called Chez Mazarin. She found it on the map. The Clean Machine was only one block away, much nearer the center of the map than yesterday—no, the day before.

Her lips trembled. It had been only one day, one change to be homeless, but it seemed much longer. If, indeed, she was not homeless still. Someone might have replaced her. Sometimes they did that. Fighting tears she stopped only briefly at the counter to pay her bill and to buy tomorrow's map before making her way home.

Inside the laundry, she opened all the machines, as she did every evening before going up the stairs. She would not have been surprised to find a note in her apartment telling her she was fired, or even to find someone else in her place, but all was as she had left it. She put the maps on the table by the door and fell into bed, grateful for the dank dampness of the sheets that told her she was in a place that she knew.

# CHAPTER 7

HER ALARM WENT off as it always did, too early. The sheets were warm and dry from her body heat. Morning sleep was precious, and she had been dreaming of that other place, that other apartment. A strange dream that seemed to make that place more familiar than this one. She huddled in the bed, half sitting up, the blankets drawn about her neck. The alarm went off again, and she cursed, bitterly but briefly. The dream had left her. She could remember nothing about it. Staggering to the bathroom, she washed her face, surprised that it looked so familiar to her. It should have been another face, with darker hair, darker eyes, a different name.

A different name? She tried, very briefly, to remember her name. Marianne something, she thought. She had it written down somewhere. While she fixed her morning eggs, she tried to remember where, but could not bring it to mind. Sighing, she put the single dish and fork into the sink, running water over them but not taking time to wash them. She had to get the machines cleaned out before the first customers arrived.

At the bottom of the stairs she paused, listening. Sometimes there were living things in the machines, and in that case emptying them could be difficult. There were no rustling or thumping noises. Encouraged, she began at the end of the row, unlatching and opening the doors that she had unlatched and opened the night before.

The indigo machine was empty. So was the green one. When she moved toward the rose washer, she heard a peculiar sound, a high-pitched whining. When the door was opened, she saw a litter of puppies lying on a pile of miscellaneous laundry. Five of them, each a different color and shape, three males, two females, all of about the same age. They half crawled, half fell out of the machine to wobble about on infant legs, tugging at her trousers and whining to be fed. She brought a bottle of milk from her apartment as well as some bread and meat scraps that all five tore at with tiny teeth, growling as they tugged and fought for possession of the best pieces. They seemed to be housebroken already, barking in treble voices to be let out. She thought of taking them to the dog pound. Surely there was a dog pound? And if there were? It could mean a half block walk or an interminable journey.

She surprised herself by finding the nearest grocery, instead, and buying a large sack of puppy kibble, wondering why she was doing it, admitting to herself at last that she was lonely. She could not remember having had that thought before, and it astonished her with its obviousness. Of course she was lonely. Why hadn't she realized that in the past? Perhaps it had been yesterday's unpleasant adventure, wandering quite alone as she had. For whatever reason, she welcomed the pups and made them a bed of a violet chenille bedspread and a bright pink tablecloth in an old fruit crate near the back door. She propped the door ajar so they could get into the weedy backyard to do their business.

She named them for their colors. Rouge, Liquorice, and Delphinium—Delphy for short—were the red, black, and blue pups. Silver and Gold were the silver-gray and yellow ones. "You can stay, at least temporarily," she told them. "And those names will do until something of your character becomes clear to me. Then I'll give you new names." She did not know where this thought came from, either. The names she had given them were adequate. Why should they need or expect new ones? Why should she?

"You need friends," something inside her spoke. "You have no friends."

She laughed. Who could have friends in this world of changing locations? Unless someone actually lived with you, in the same house, one day's neighbor could become another day's foreigner, adrift in some remote suburb.

When she closed the laundry to go for tomorrow's map, the puppies barked behind her, demandingly, then trailed at her heels in an untidy kite's tail of staggering doglets as she walked them three blocks to the kiosk and back.

"There's no excuse for not getting one's map," she confided. "There's always a kiosk within six blocks. It's arranged that way. If one doesn't get a map, it's because one is simply too scatterbrained."

"Or ill," her mind suggested with a discomforting and unusual percipience. "Or busy, or unconscious, or held prisoner, or crippled, or old, or drunk, or not very bright."

"Too scatterbrained," she said firmly. "We have ours, don't we?"

There was scattered agreement from five small throats. Already she was beginning to see differences among them. Liquorice was going to be smooth-haired and large—he had huge feet. Rouge was going to be fluffy. The tips of his ears barely showed above his puff of fur, and he had a tightly curled tail. The yellow female tended to be a slinker, a peerer from corners and under chairs, with curious and suspicious brown eyes. The blue-gray one was afraid of nothing, and would have fur as sleek as lizard skin. The silver-gray one was quiet and thoughtful. She had this habit of looking wisely at Marianne, without blinking.

"I have no idea why they run things this way," she told the puppy, sure she had asked a question about the city of Varnatur. "It's always been this way."

Though Marianne seemed to remember a place where things had stayed the same. Oh, the joyous recognition of a place like that. To see the same faces, the same places. To know them! Not always to be among strange places and people.

It was an aberrant thought. One she might be punished for, if anyone found out.

"The Map Police could find out," she told the puppies. "They really could. They know things about people. Sometimes they come into the laundry and arrest people. For the things they're trying to clean, you know?"

Silver looked at her with complete understanding, as though she knew all too well.

Usually in the evening, Marianne watched the television. There were always three music programs, two drama programs, and the obligatory palace broadcast, in no consistent order. There was also the half-hour lost-and-found program, which she always watched with complete attention. It wasn't the mappers' fault: every program started with a disclaimer by the map commission, but sometimes things got disconnected. Children from their parents. Husbands and wives. Parts of houses. Belongings.

First there was a fanfare. Then the disclaimer, read by the High Commissioner. Then the brief announcements, sometimes with pictures. "Reward offered for the return of our beloved son, Roger Erickson, age three, lost during the last changeover." Name of family, name of house. Marianne wrote it down. She always wrote the locations down. Who knew? She might find one of them. Picture of Roger. Fat. Dimpled. Not very bright looking.

"Not very bright looking," said Marianne.

"Woof," agreed Rouge.

"Reward offered for the location of our kitchen and servants' quarters, inadvertently misplaced during the last changeover." Name of house. Floor plan of kitchen, as though that made any difference. "If you found a kitchen attached to your house and it didn't belong there," Marianne remarked, "you'd call them, wouldn't you? Why show us the floor plan?"

Gold panted briefly, licked a paw, then returned her liquid brown gaze to Marianne's face.

"Reward offered for a set of five things taken from the palace," the announcer intoned. "Purposefully detached, not lost during changeover. All citizens are encouraged to keep their eyes open for five things that may have been stolen from the palace. Five similar things."

Silver growled deep in her throat. Rouge laughed. Delphy tried to catch his tail. Gold and Liquorice were playing tag around the legs of a chair.

"No," Marianne said, looking at them. "Puppies aren't things. The announcement said five things."

"Not many things come in fives," her mind said.

"No," she said again. "Puppies aren't things. It couldn't be.

# CHAPTER 8

TODAY'S CITY WAS Brandton-Minor. Marianne checked the map over her morning coffee. The palace was at the center of the map, as it always was. Other things moved; the palace did not. Not the palace and not the Bureau of Maps. The Clean Machine had continued its slow approach and was now within six blocks of it. "We'll probably never be this close again," she told the pups. "We can go see the palace this evening. After work. I'll get tomorrow's map at noon, and that'll leave plenty of time." It seemed likely that palace viewing would need an hour or more. The television often showed endless streams of pedestrians and bus passengers on their way to or from the palace.

When she set out, the puppies in a straggling tail at her heels, the streets were full of people headed in the same direction. Marianne followed along, part of the human procession, smiling, nodding, exchanging a few words. Today she was tempted to look for someone recognizable. Someone she might have seen before. Marianne played this game seldom and saw anyone she recognized less often yet, but she frequently met the same half-curious, half-searching glances she knew was on her own face.

The block nearest the palace fence was very crowded. The puppies whined. Marianne picked them up and put them in the large canvas bag she was carrying. Their heads poked above the top, peering curiously at the crowd.

People worked their way to the fence, stood there staring for a time, then departed. Those at the back of the crowd were gradually shifted forward. When Marianne's time at the fence came, she stared no less curiously than the rest. There was the sloping lawn, the two vast fountain basins to left and right, the slender pillars supporting the roof of the portico, the rows of flimsy trees. A line of black-clad guardsmen stood motionlessly upon the stairs. A gardener worked on his knees beside one of the fountains.

One of the puppies whined, briefly, and there was a small convulsion in the canvas bag. Marianne looked down to see the bag almost empty. Only Rouge and Liquorice stared up at her, their tongues out. The others had jumped out and run off. Somewhere.

"Cute pups," someone said.

She looked through the fence into the eyes of a guardsman, his face immobile, as though carved from some dark stone. One hand held a leash from which a dog leaned toward the fence, straining, teeth exposed in an eager, hungry dog smile. "I will bite you if I get a chance," the smile said. "They will reward me if I do it well."

"How many of them do you have?" the guardsman asked in a significant voice.

She started to say "Five," then choked the word off as Rouge barked a treble puppy bark and nipped at Liquorice's ear. "This is Rouge," Marianne said weakly. "This is Liquorice."

He nodded, moving off down the row of spectators. At the far, right-hand corner of the palace was a low tower, crowned with a row of arched and curtained windows. One of the curtains twitched as though someone had been standing behind it, watching.

Marianne turned away. She wanted to look for Gold and Silver and Delphy, but something told her it would be dangerously foolish to do so just now. The place felt like the streets did just before change, shivering with purpose. Something impended. She hurried away through the crowd, slowing as it thinned in order not to draw attention to herself.

There were only a few blocks to traverse, back to the laundry. As she turned the last corner, she noted half consciously that the street was empty, an unusual thing for this time of night. It was not until she had come halfway from the corner, however, that they stepped out of an alley and came toward her.

Their hair was stiffened into spikes and dyed in shades of bright green or purple or blue. Their faces were painted. She stopped where she was, thought of running, knew it would do no good. Her money belt was at home. They would take her wallet, but she could spare that. If that was all they took. . . .

"Hey, mama," the largest of them said. His voice was silky, insinuating, a rapist's voice. "Hey, lady. Hey, you. Where you goin'?"

It would do no good to talk. Talking would only make it worse. If she could stay on the street, likely they would not kill her. The Map Police did not like people being killed on the street. She was silent, quiet, holding the bag across her chest like a shield.

His name was written on his forehead in blue ink. Ironballs. Fanning out behind him were Blueshit and Wrecker, their names tattooed above the brows in purple and red, and a huge, muscular woman with her name on both cheeks, Brasstits. Her gilded nipples thrust through holes in a leather vest.

Rouge whined, pawed at the edge of the sack, overbalanced and dropped to the sidewalk with an abrupt half-bark of surprise.

"Hey, she's got puppies," said the woman in a narrow, nasal voice which was so surprised it was for the moment nonthreatening. "Pups!"

"His name is Rouge," Marianne found the voice to say. "The other one is Liquorice."

"Where'd you get 'em?" Ironballs asked in a mild tone.

"I guess they were abandoned," she said, trying to keep her voice from trembling. "I found them."

"In an alley, huh?" he said, almost sympathetically. She did not correct him. She didn't want them to know where she lived, or worked. She merely nodded, not moving. Liquorice tried to climb out of the bag and she set him down beside Rouge.

"We could eat 'em," offered Blueshit. "I ate dog once."

"You'd eat shit," Brasstits offered mildly. "You'd cut off your mother's tit and eat that. Trouble with you, Blue, is you got no discrimination."

Rouge, moving with unpuppylike speed, darted toward the alley entrance from which the mapless ones had emerged. With a shout, half of amusement, half of challenge, Brasstits turned and pursued him, Blueshit and Wrecker close behind, whooping with glee. Ironballs stayed where he was, eyeing Marianne as though he planned to butcher her for the pot. "What you got good, Mama? Got money? Love or money, which? Huh? Maybe both?" He raped her with his eyes, an anticipatory revel.

Liquorice barked briefly, lifted his infant leg and peed on the man's boots. Ironballs let out a yell of rage and snatched at the pup who darted just out of reach, toward the alley.

"Go home," said a voice in Marianne's ear. "Go home, fast."

Ironballs was chasing Liquorice; the others of the gang were chasing Rouge. For the moment, none of them was watching her. Marianne got into the laundry and double-locked the door, then stood in the dark, watching the street through a crack in the shutter.

A sound drew her attention from the window. All five of the pups were sitting behind her in a line, watching her watching the street. Rouge and Liquorice had somehow rejoined the others.

Out in the street, the four mapless ones emerged from the alley once more to stare up and down the street, waving their arms and cursing one another loudly for the loss of their prey.

"Thank you," said Marianne.

"You're welcome," said the voice in her mind.

She looked into Gold's eyes, seeing something there of comprehension. "You said that?" she challenged.

"Woof," Gold replied in a puppyish treble, licking her front paw. "Woof."

The following morning, the Clean Machine was only a block from the palace. Marianne felt this was uncomfortably close. Too near the center of things. Early in the morning people started flowing toward the palace grounds; all day the crowds pushed to and fro, ripple-mobs of people ebbing and flowing. Her first customer of the day was a talkative old man with a cane. He had an ancient curve-topped trunk to be laundered.

"Got to frettin' me," he said, counting out the coins that the chart gave as the correct charge for luggage—one piece, footlocker or larger. "Don't know what might be in there. All kinds of memories, most likely. Things I don't want to rake up. Thought I'd launder it first." He peered curiously about him, inspecting every corner of the place, taking a tottery step or two to look into Marianne's little office, committing it to memory. The eyes he turned on her were keen and youthful in the wrinkled face.

"We're very glad to take care of it for you," Marianne murmured, maneuvering her loading cart through the door to the curb where the bus driver had dropped the trunk. "We'll just put it here for the indigo washer as soon as this cycle's complete."

"People in there?" he asked as she reentered with the trunk. "Seem to hear them yellin' about somethin'."

"No," she answered absentmindedly. "As a matter of fact, that's a mixed load. Two parrots from the pet store down the block and a set of encyclopedias. A mother brought the books in. Before she gives them to her children."

"Ah," he nodded wisely. "Stuff she doesn't want the kiddy widdles to know, most likely. My ma was the same way. We knew all about it from the kids at school and watchin' the farm animals, but she'd have it we was innocent as daisies. Well. Mamas are like that."

"Are they?" Marianne asked. It was one of those bits of conversation that annoyed her, often keeping her awake at night. Were mamas like that? How did he know? And if he knew, why didn't she?

"Most of 'em," he confided, sitting down on one of the uncomfortable chairs and pulling a folded newspaper from his pocket. "Says here there's going to be rain this summer."

"Is there?"

"Yep. Says so here. Says the royal family's goin' on a tour. Foreign parts. The Queen and the Duke of Eyes."

This was another thing that annoyed her. Foreign parts. Other places. Where? Why had she never thought of going? Why had she never met anyone who had gone? And who was the Duke of Eyes? His picture was not in any of the royal portraits she had hung in the office. Queen, King, the Jack of Japes, Lady Ten. No Duke at all.

The buzzer on the indigo washer went off with an ear-shattering shriek. Marianne shut it off hastily and opened the door. The two parrots emerged, damp and disheveled, to perch on the dryer door and complain at her. There seemed to be nothing left of the set of encyclopedias.

"Thought that'd happen," the old man said, rising to help her get the trunk into the machine. "That's the trouble with things in writin'. Sometimes you take one little word away and the whole thing falls apart. Ever notice that?"

Marianne thrust the trunk into the machine, set the dials, and turned purposefully toward the parrots. They, meantime, had flown up to one of the light fixtures and regarded her with disfavor from that lofty height.

"Quite dry enough, thank you," one of them offered. "As is my friend."

"You're dripping all over the floor," Marianne observed.

"As would you," said the other parrot, regarding her warily, "if you had been forcibly immersed in that monster. I want to say something but can't remember what."

"That's what the laundering was for," the first parrot reminded him. "Language."

"I'd forgotten," said the second. "Isn't that astonishing. Well, though I seem to be unable to remember the proper words, whatever vile and insulting language best suits the occasion, Miss, consider it said." He began to preen himself with ostentatious fervor as Marianne and the old man watched, eyes wide.

"Thought I'd walk over and see the palace," the old man observed, "while that washes."

"Feel free to do so," she remarked absently. "I'll put it in the dryer for you." Silver had come into the room and appeared to be in silent conversation with the parrots, a colloquy of gesture, paw taps, wing shrugs, head twistings. As the old man left, the pet shop woman came to fetch her birds, a cage in either hand, and as she left a guardsman entered, his shiny little eyes peering into every corner of the room.

"Name?" he asked, flipping open a notebook.

"The Clean Machine," she said, mouth open in astonishment. There had never been a guardsman in the laundry before.

"No, lovey, your name."

"Marianne," she replied. "Just Marianne."

"Well, Just Marianne, this is a routine procedure. Each day we investigate all premises within three blocks of the palace. Lookin' for anarchists and revolutionaries, so they tell us, not that we've ever found any. Found a nest of revisionists once, but nobody cared."

"What were they revising?" she asked, truly curious.

"Don't know. Didn't ask 'em. Now. This is a cleaning establishment, right? You the proprietor?"

"No," she admitted. "I'm only the manager."

"Live on the premises?"

"There's an apartment upstairs."

"Married? Cohabiting? Children?"

"No." She started to mention the dogs, but then was quite unaccountably silent.

"Where were you yesterday?"

"About six blocks away," she admitted. "I went to look at the palace after closing time."

"Quite a sight, isn't it?"

No, she thought, even as her head nodded polite agreement. It wasn't much of a sight, really. There hadn't been that much to see. She didn't say it. He wrote busily in his book for a moment, starting as the buzzer on the indigo machine went off.

"What in hell!"

"It's just the machine," she explained. "Excuse me. I have to take the trunk out." But when she opened the machine, she could not take the trunk out. It had vanished, in that unaccountable way in which things intended for cleaning sometimes did vanish, as though they were held together by dirt, by a kind of ephemeral filth that could be dismissed by water and soap. Of course, things sometimes reappeared, as well. Reconstituted, one might say. She stared into the washer, waiting for the trunk to emerge. In its place were five velvet cushions, sodden and steaming, a gemmed crown on each, glittering like malignant octopus eyes from a watery cave.

"Aha," said the guardsman. "Got you."

The cell in which they left her was not uncomfortable. There was a cot, a toilet, a basin, a glass for drinking water, even a screen so she could use the facilities without undue display to anyone peering in through the little grated window. The room was reasonably warm, and it was dry. On a table by the heavy door, barred with iron and studded with thick nails of gleaming bronze, the five crowns huddled like socialites in a drunk tank, making a fierce show of quality to cow whomever was responsible for the outrage.

Marianne was no longer looking at them. She had looked, for a time, trying to remember if she had indeed stolen any such thing, for this is what she was accused of. She had tried to explain to the guardsman that the crowns were not unlike the elephant harness or the double bed, having arrived in some similar and as unexplainable a fashion, but he had been unwilling to entertain any such possibility.

"You were at the palace, you admit it," he had said.

"Only out by the fence. Along with hundreds of other people."

"But you were there. And five things disappeared, and now you have five things."

What could she say to that? She did, indeed, have them. Even now she had them. "The broadcast didn't say what things," she pleaded. "It didn't say what things at all!"

He sneered, pointing. Could anyone doubt that crowns like these belonged in a palace? Could anyone doubt they had no business in the indigo washer at the Clean Machine?

Marianne sank onto the cot. She wondered if the old man had

ever come back for his trunk. She wondered if crying would help. She wondered if screaming would help and decided it would not; the sound of screaming had echoed through the prison almost since she had entered it, sometimes softly and plaintively, sometimes with an access of agony that made it quite unbearable to hear.

"But I didn't take them," she said again, aloud.

"You're not charged with taking them," said a voice. "You're charged with receiving them."

There was someone at the grated window, peering in at her. She could see one glassy eye. "I didn't receive them," she said. "The machine did. It does things like that."

"You'll have a chance to explain that to the magistrates, tomorrow," said the voice. "I thought I'd warn you, in case you wanted to change your clothes and tidy up a bit."

"I only have these clothes," she shouted, suddenly angry. "The ones I had on."

"Closet," said the voice. "There's a closet."

Of course there was a closet. It contained three pairs of overalls, a fireman's helmet, and a ball gown at least five sizes too large. "I will appear before the magistrates as I am," she said aloud, attempting to sound dignified. "In my own clothes." She was wearing a simple shirtwaist dress, now somewhat rumpled, and a wool sweater, both in mud shades.

The grating across the window in the cell door slammed shut, as though in frustration.

The five puppies came out from beneath her cot and gathered around her feet.

"This is ridiculous," she said. "How did I ever get into this mess? How did you get in here?"

# CHAPTER 9

THE MAGISTRATES WERE informal in their treatment of those brought before them. There were seven chairs on the dais, and occasionally all seven of them were occupied, though usually only two or three of the magistrates were seated there at a time, often at least one of them asleep. The others wandered about the courtroom or left the room entirely and could occasionally be heard ordering someone around backstage, as it were. One magistrate played endless games of chess with himself. Another drew endless pictures of naked women without heads. Only the tall, dark woman at the left end of the row seemed to pay attention.

"Window dressing," said the voice in Marianne's mind. "She's the only real one. The others are merely window dressing." The dark woman peered at her out of fiery eyes, hot, eager eyes, belying her casual demeanor.

"Just Marianne, charged with receiving stolen goods," the prosecutor intoned, tugging at the wig that seemed always about to slip off the back of his bald head. "Material of national importance, stolen from the palace."

"Trial by combat," the dark woman drawled in a bored though somehow elated voice. "Next case."

# CHAPTER 10

"YOU HAVE UNTIL the holiday to obtain a champion," the voice said through the grate in the window. "I told you you should have cleaned yourself up. The Queen thought your disheveled state was disrespectful."

"The Queen?"

"You should feel honored. She heard your case personally."

"Who did?"

"The Queen."

"Not that I saw!"

"Oh, you must have seen her. A dark woman, very slender. With fiery eyes."

"One of the magistrates was a dark woman."

"First magistrate of the realm, the Queen is."

"She didn't hear my case! She didn't hear anything but the charge! She didn't even give me a chance to plead guilty or not guilty."

"Oh, she knew you were guilty. It's just a case of deciding punishment, don't you know."

A tiny growl came from beneath the bunk. Marianne interpreted this as a warning and said nothing more about her innocence. "Where am I supposed to get a champion! I don't know anyone."

"Then you'll have to fight the Duke of Eyes yourself. Not, by the way, something I would choose to do on a holiday afternoon."

"I don't even know who he is!"

"The Queen's champion, of course. Who else would he be?" The grating slammed closed. This anonymous informant always slammed the grating to end conversation, as though the very act of conversing led to unbearable frustration or annoyance. Marianne reviewed what she had said—certainly nothing to offend. The behavior of the grating voice had no logic to it. It told her things she did not ask to hear and seemed to expect some response she could not give. She lay down on the cot, hearing the scrabble of puppy feet beneath it. They had found some way to enter and leave the cell—some way she could not find though she had searched for hours—but they always hid when anyone was at the door. "I don't know what's happening," she whispered as a moist little tongue explored between her fingers. "I'm terrified, and I don't know what's happening."

# CHAPTER 11

"I HOPE YOU know what you're doing," Ellat said, picking up her teacup and pausing in the doorway as though wanting both to go and to stay. Behind her in the vaulted room, Makr Avehl frowned at her as he adjusted the sleeves of his ceremonial robe and sat down on the narrow bed.

"Of course I don't, Ellat. No more than I did last time. But I have at least as good a clue this time as I had then. She has the bracelet, and I can follow that. Also, this time there are momentary gods. They will certainly have trailed after her, and they will have left a track. Surely someone as skilled as I am reputed to be can sniff them out." He shrugged in self deprecation, giving her a boyish smile.

"What makes you think . . ." she began in a maternal voice, then made a fretful motion and said, "oh, never mind. It's just all so . . . uncertain."

"You want to know what makes me think the woman washing clothes is the operative symbol? A hunch, Ellat. And your favorite at the Cave, the one with the scary eyes."

"Therat?"

"Yes. That one. She agrees that the symbol is very potent. So, for all intents and purposes, I'm looking for a laundress. I shall put myself into the proper frame of mind. I shall burn the right incense,'' he gestured at the ceremonial brazier beside the bed, already wreathed in smoke. "I shall recite the correct words and send my spirit self looking for a laundress. A laundress, mind you, with five dogs of five colors. I'll grant you there may be more than one set of beings meeting that description, but not many more than one.''

"You're not taking Aghrehond?''

"I would if he were here, Ellat, but he's either on his way home or still in New York. He may be here by morning. Perhaps he'll come after me as he did last time. I'll leave it to him. He certainly carried the brunt of the battle during our last foray against Madame. And he had all the best of it. He appeared more or less as himself while I—well, I was undoubtedly a monster.''

"Good-hearted, however,'' Ellat interjected. "You must have been good-hearted.''

"Some part of me may have been,'' he agreed somberly. "She gave me that role last time, an equivocal one, because she did not know how she felt about me. This time I will choose what role to take. I shall go this time as something every maiden dreams of.'' He laughed, sardonically.

"What's that?''

"Why, Ellat. You were a maiden once. Can't you guess?''

"You don't mean . . .''

He waved to her, a small wave, dismissive as well as affectionate, as he lay down on the cot. "I do mean, love. Wish me luck.''

# CHAPTER 12

IN THE DUNGEON, Marianne huddled on the hard cot, her eyes shut, trying to dream of that other place, trying desperately to pretend she was somewhere else.

"Hsss," a low whisper at her ear. "Hsss."

She turned her head toward the wall, feeling the faintest breath against her cheek. Mortar had fallen from between two of the cyclopean stones of the dungeon wall, leaving a narrow slot through which the breath came, a fervent little wind, hot and smelling of grease and garlic.

"Hsss, can you hear me?"

She put her lips within an inch of the wall. "Yes, I can hear you."

"What are you in for?"

"Receiving stolen goods. Palace goods."

"Ah. They'll probably hang you, then. Or feed you to the plants in the botanical garden. Queen Luby likes to do that. I'm in for sedition."

"How long have you been here?"

"Haven't any idea. Don't even remember coming here. Just woke up here one day. Isn't it that way with everyone?"

A chill began just above Marianne's eyes, moving swiftly

down her body to her toes, tingling along her arms. Within her mind something turned sluggishly, as though in drugged slumber, deeply somnolent and yet restless. The combination of cold and the vertiginous shifting within herself made her nauseated, and she gagged. What the voice said was true. She couldn't remember where she had been before. She couldn't remember coming to . . . to whatever town this was. Surely she couldn't always have worked for the laundry. "What did you do before?" she begged of the wall, seeking a clue to her own past. Surely she had a past!

"Advertising," it answered promptly, perhaps with a touch of pride. "Something to do with advertising. Insurance, I think. Or perhaps toothpaste."

"They don't seem similar."

"Identical," the voice hissed as though from some great distance. "Actually, they're identical."

She felt the source of the voice had withdrawn, though only temporarily, and this assumption was verified in a moment when it resumed. "Had to check the corridor. They spy, you know. They sneak the gratings open and stand there, listening. Always check the grating before you say anything."

"I don't have anything bad to say," she objected.

"Oh, they don't care. Bad. Good. It doesn't matter. They'll use it against you anyhow. Where were we?"

"They say I have to have a trial by combat," she blurted. "With the Duke of Eyes. I don't know what it means."

A long silence. A sound as of lips smacking, or it could be a tsking; malice or sympathy, impossible to tell which. "Well, they won't hang you or feed you to the plants, then, which is too bad."

"Bad? Not to be fed to the plants?" she demanded.

"Ever seen him?" the voice asked. "The Duke?"

"No."

"He's sort of a machine, you know. Only a tiny part human. Like his body doesn't . . . function. So he's in this machine. And they keep changing it. One time he'll have hooks for hands and the next time, kind of grabbers. Or clubs. And one time he'll have legs, but the next time tracks, like some kind of big earth mover. He doesn't talk. Just looks at you with his eyes. Wherever his eyes look, that's where the machine goes. Whatever his mind thinks, that's what the machine does. And it's big, you know. About twelve feet high.''

"What kind of a champion could fight that?" she asked, holding her terror at arm's length. "How could I fight that?"

"Well, you can't, of course. Best thing to do is lie down, put your head on your arms and let him kill you. Not many people can do that, of course. He plays. Whips. Pincers. Things like that. It hurts, and it's hard not to run and leap and try to escape. That's what people come for, of course. To see the opponent try to escape.''

"In other words," she whispered, "a trial by combat with the Duke of Eyes is really just another way of saying someone is to be publicly tortured to death?''

"Well . . ." the voice faded away. There was a distant clanging, a sound of several voices raised, a long silence. Then the hissing once more, close, very close, "That's what it amounts to, Marianne.''

She had not told the voice her name. She rolled away from the aperture, fighting her welling nausea, knowing it wasn't a prisoner who spoke to her through that rent in the masonry. Or, if a prisoner, then one who had been put up to it by someone else. By the nameless voice that spoke through the grating. By the dark woman on the magistrate's bench. By the Queen. By someone who wanted to be sure she knew what would happen. Someone who wanted to savor her terror.

A soft nose pushed into her palm. A moist tongue licked at it, a puppy voice whined.

"They're going to kill me," she said, hopelessly. "That's what this has all been about. They're going to kill me. And I don't even know why."

# CHAPTER 13

In Alphenlicht, Makr Avehl lay silently on the narrow cot, eyes closed, his breathing so shallow he appeared hardly to breathe at all. Around him extended a gray vacancy that was brushed intermittently with hints of color, echoing occasionally with a distant sound, a melody, perhaps a voice. It smelled of mossy woods, then of cinnamon, then of something namelessly disgusting. He had the sensation of walking, or swimming, or perhaps flying through this nameless void, reaching out with his senses toward a potent symbol. It was a familiar quest. He had floated here before, very recently. It was only a few weeks ago that he had followed the other *Marianne* into the false worlds that opened upon this nothingness, the dream worlds, the fantasy worlds that clustered within and beside and through the worlds of reality.

What would it be this time? One of Madame's worlds, certainly, and yet not wholly hers. Each time she drew a victim into one of her worlds, whether purposely or unwittingly, that victim would change the world, little or much. Marianne's presence would have modified the world in which she found herself, would have changed it and put a mark upon it that the follower might seek as a trailfinder seeks a cairn.

A woman washing clothes. The slap of sodden fabric. The slosh of water. The soggy enervation of steam. The fatty stink of soap. He turned his head on the pillow, evoking and following that fragrance. The smell of soap. He seemed to scent it, far off, coming closer. And a sound, as of some great tumble of waters. Thrashing. Gushing. A whirling sound.

He drifted. Drifted uncomfortably. Wet. Very wet. His whole body was soaked. He choked, drowning, forgetting, screaming at the dark thundering waters around him.

Someone opened the door of the indigo washer and he spilled onto the floor, wet as a flounder, his princely garb reeking of bleach.

"Gracious," said the old man across the crook of his cane. "It's Prince Charming! I thought you might be my trunk, coming back."

"I've come to rescue the fair damsel," The Prince gargled, gasping for air. "Where is she?"

"If you're talking about Marianne," the old man answered, "She's imprisoned." He nodded, his head tilting to and fro like a rocking chair sent into motion by some constant breeze, moving of itself, unable to stop. "Sentenced to trial by combat. The whole town is talking of nothing else."

The Prince rose with what dignity he could muster. His satin trousers leaked dye even as they shrank into sausage-skin tightness. Rust bloomed on the hilt of his sword all at once, like a flower. His velvet cape was a rag, ripped into fragments by the waters. He cursed.

"You must be her champion," the old man commented, gesturing as he did so at the great machine across the aisle. "The indigo dryer," he murmured, staring at Prince Charming's trousers. "I'd recommend it."

# CHAPTER 14

IN THE MIDDLE of the night, the voice returned, hissing once more between the impenetrable stones. "Marianne. Marianne." Insinuating as a serpent. "Marianne? Your champion has arrived."

It was impossible to ignore the voice, even though she told herself it was a ploy, a feint, an attempt to give her hope that would then be dashed. She tried to keep silent and could not. "Who?" she begged. "Who is it?"

"Prince Charming," said the voice with a lewd giggle. "All got up for the part."

She turned away from the wall and put her arm across her eyes, willing herself not to cry, not to speak. The little grating opened and someone peered in. She kept her eyes shut, breathed slowly, pretended to be asleep.

"You'll meet him next holiday!" the voice exulted. "At the colosseum. In the catacombs where the victims are prepared!"

Marianne didn't answer. She could not have answered. In this nightmare world, she could only endure for a time, then die. What was the point in argument or expostulation? What was the point of anything?

Slow tears crept down her face, hidden behind her arm. After a time, the grating slammed shut, as though in pique.

# CHAPTER 15

PRINCE CHARMING WAS hiding in an alley near the palace, hoping very strongly that the gang of mapless ones he had recently evaded would not find him again. He had had to fight off two such gangs already, and his rusty sword was proving to be of little help. He carried it in his hand, unsheathed, since if it was sheathed when he needed it, there was a strong likelihood it could not be pulled free at all. Once dry, he had assumed he would be able to obtain clothing, directions, perhaps a hot meal or a warm bed, all those things that civilized men take more or less for granted. His first disillusionment had come when he approached a store which purported, by the terms of its window displays and name, to sell clothing.

"Y'got a coupon?" the clerk had asked him curiously when Makr Avehl had asked to see something in a cloak and tights, size forty-two long.

"Coupon?"

"A coupon entitlin' you to go around in fancy dress like that there. I mean, I'm not goin' to say nothin' to the Map Police, they'll find you soon enough in that getup, Mack, but it'd be my job if I sold you somethin' like that without a coupon."

Prince Charming sighed. He felt it would be unbecoming to succumb to local pressure in the matter of dress, but one could not go about the streets looking like a derelict. "How about a regular sports coat and slacks, then. Shirt size sixteen-and-a-half, thirty-two."

"Fine. Y'got the money?"

Prince Charming laid gems and gold upon the counter.

"I didn't ask did you have no joolry. I asked did you have money. Like coin of the realm, like moolah, like voskies, double-voskies or maybe a ten vosky bill. I can't do nothing with those."

Prince Charming asked the way to a pawn shop or exchange bank and encountered the realities of the city.

"Listen, Mack. You can't find nothin' without you got a map. First thing you got to do is lay your hands on tomorrow's map, got that? Then you can find yourself some pawn shop or whatever."

A few incisive questions asked of passersby elicited the information that maps were available at kiosks or twenty-four-hour restaurants for one vosky the map.

Prince Charming repaired to the nearest restaurant he could find and asked for a job as dishwasher.

"It'd have to be that, wouldn't it," said the manager, staring at him with obvious distaste. "You sure couldn't wait tables in that getup. Yeah, I suppose you can wash dishes. One vosky an hour and your supper. Y'got your work permit?"

"Work permit?" asked Prince Charming.

A few incisive questions asked of the restaurant manager gave the Prince the information that work permits were issued at the palace, between the hours of eight a.m. and noon each day.

"Where will I find the palace?" the Prince asked, exiting the restaurant a few moments later to the sound of raucous laughter.

"It seems to me," mused the Prince to himself, "that there is something wickedly illogical at work here."

He found a television store and watched the broadcast of the palace viewing. During the broadcast, the announcer used the phrase, "Here at the center of the city." Sighing, Prince

Charming set out to find the center of the city, by trial and error.

By nightfall, he had worked his way within three blocks of the palace. Not wishing to draw himself to the attention of the guards, he took refuge in an alley, intending to apply for a work permit in the morning. When he awoke, he found himself in a different alley, with the palace nowhere in sight. He had not eaten in two days.

The Prince decided to beg a meal. He was promptly set upon by the Map Police and thrashed before being given a stern warning. Begging was not permitted in Bimbleton. The Prince decided to scavenge a meal. This brought him to the attention of the first of the mapless gangs.

"That trash can, in case you're interested, joker, is in our territory." The speaker had green hair and his name tattooed on his forehead. Bonecracker.

"I'm sorry," said the Prince. "I didn't know trash cans were anybody's territory."

"He didn't know," Bonecracker advised his friends, Dangerous and Lethal. "Ain't that a pity. He didn't know."

The Prince tried his sword and found it locked in the sheath. He therefore leapt straight upward and caught the bottom rung of a fire escape which lowered itself under his weight into the waiting arms of the trio. The Prince gave an excellent accounting of himself with the sheathed sword, emerging with one black eye, a split lip, and assorted bruises around the ribs and belly. Dangerous had, as he recommended to Lethal and Bonecracker, split. The other two were stretched beside the disputed trash can, which, on examination, proved to be empty. Another can, further down the block, yielded half a sack of potato chips and an unopened flip-top can of Ruby García's Bean Dip with extra jalapeños.

Later that day he found a public drinking fountain and stayed near it for some time, attempting to put out the fire in his stomach. By evening he had worked his way to the palace once more. Moving as casually as his strange garb, now further battle-worn, would allow, he found a place near the fence that was partially hidden by the overhanging limbs of a large tree. When the tremor of change came, he grasped the iron fence and held tight, emerging from the changeover still on the sidewalk adjacent to the palace.

Satisfied, he evaded a mapless gang set upon stealing his sword and found the nearby alley previously referred to in which to spend the rest of the night.

"Work permit, sure," said the palace functionary the next morning, polishing the brass buttons on his cuff. "Y'got entry papers?"

"Entry papers?" said the Prince in a dignified voice with overtones of distress. "Entry papers?"

"Apply for those at the Bureau of Maps. Be sure to have your vaccination documents, three letters of reference from local residents, and the quota number under which you entered the country."

"Quota number," said the Prince vaguely, beginning to get the idea.

When next violently approached by members of a mapless gang, Prince Charming asserted with a bare though rusty blade his intention of joining them. Brasstits believed it was because of her well displayed charms. Ironballs thought it was because of his obvious leadership capabilities. In reality, Prince Charming would have joined anyone he thought able to provide him with a decent meal and some idea of what was going on.

"Why don't we . . . ah . . . rip off a map vendor?" he asked. "Then we'd know where we wanted to go tomorrow."

Brasstits shook her head pityingly. She was drawn to this peculiar stranger, partly because he obviously needed mothering and partly because he was so—oh, polite. Most men—well, no need to go into that, but they didn't act like this one did. "You poor jerk," she said. "That's not the way it works."

Prince Charming smiled up at her from under his lashes. He was not above flirtation for a good purpose, though he had not used this particular technique since age ten. "How does it work, Brassy? Tell me."

"If you don't buy a map for one vosky, the map just falls apart. You can't steal one. You can't peek over anybody's shoulder, either, or the Map Police'll put your eyes out. You could find somebody's got a map and offer to cohabit, if you want to, but the people who're willing to do that are pretty repulsive, let me tell you.''

"So, if you can't buy a map, you don't know where you are. If you can't get a job, you can't buy a map. If you can't get a work permit, you can't get a job. If you don't have entry papers, you can't get a work permit. If you don't have local references, you can't get entry papers, and you can't get local references without having a map. Is that more or less it?''

"More or less," she said admiringly. "You catch on fast.''

"Which is why there are mapless ones, I guess. You've learned to do without.''

"Well, it's either that or the arena. I mean, you can volunteer to be a victim for the arena, to fight the Duke of Eyes, and they'll feed you and take care of you until the next game comes up.''

"Duke of Eyes?" asked the Prince with a shiver of foreboding. "Duke of Eyes?''

Brasstits described the Duke with loving attention to the more formidable details. "Like, he gets to fight the victims, you know. And he gets to fight the champions, too. Like there's this girl, Marianne, and she has a champion going to fight for her. I'd like to see that. He won't get anywhere with the Duke of Eyes, let me tell you.''

The Prince sighed, his worst fears fulfilled. "Where will this take place, Brassy? And when?''

Once the Prince had the day-to-day details of survival under control—though he was unable to do anything about improving his clothing—he worked his way to the palace once more and announced himself as Marianne's champion. He asked to see the Fair Maiden and was greeted with a chorus of jeering laughter.

"Whadaya think this is, the Love Boat?" a functionary asked him. "You get to fight for her, chum, not canoodle with her.''

"I didn't have canoodling in mind," said the Prince in a very dignified voice. "I simply thought I should meet her and assure her of my best efforts. She may not even know I've arrived.''

"Oh, she knows!" There was laughter again. "You can see her at the arena, buddy. If you can find it." There was more hooting laughter, and the Prince left the palace feeling quite downhearted.

"How would you find the arena, if you had to?" he asked Ironballs.

"Gosh, I dunno," said Ironballs. "It moves around, the arena does, just like everyplace else. Brasstits, how'd you find the arena if you had to?"

"Find somebody that was goin' there, I guess," she said. "Maybe you could do that."

Two days later, Prince Charming awoke in front of a pawn shop.

He took the gems and gold he had hidden in his left boot heel and spread them upon the dirty counter.

"My, my, look at that," the pawnshop owner gazed at the glittering hoard. "Where'd you get all this, man?"

"It's mine," said the Prince. "Not stolen."

"I didn't suppose it was. Just interested is all. What you want for 'em?"

"Clothing," said the Prince. "Voskies."

The pawnshop owner shook his head. "Sorry. Can't give you anything but coupons. Look through the coupon book if you like. If you see anything there you can use, let me know."

The coupon book was dusty. Most of the coupons were handwritten. One offered a home-cooked meal, another to repair a saddle. One offered two nights' lodging with Mrs. McAlister. One offered to tell his fortune.

"I'd like the meal and the lodging," said the Prince. "If that includes a bath."

"Not unless it says so," the pawnshop owner shook his head. "I doubt Mrs. McAlister would let you in, the way you look and smell. Tell you what. Why'nt you take the meal and the fortune. I'll sell you those two for this littlest jewel, right here."

"I don't need my fortune told," said the Prince. "I already know how things are going."

"Yeah, but I'm throwing it in. Won't cost you anything."

The Prince took the coupon, was directed to the house where the meal was offered—corned beef and cabbage and pecan pie for dessert—and then to Madame Fifi's Emporium of Truth.

"Trouble with you is," said Fifi, "you got body odor."

"So would you," snarled Prince Charming, "if you'd been

sleeping in alleys and eating out of trash cans for the past week.''

''You know, that's a very good observation,'' she remarked, rubbing her hands gently over the crystal ball. ''I probably would smell pretty bad. Of course this is your fortune we're doing here, so how I might smell under any circumstances at all is what you might tend to call kind of irrelevant.''

''That's so,'' admitted the Prince.

''Let's see here. You gotta dangerous trial comin' up in the near future. You gotta rescue a Fair Maiden. Lord love a duck, it's been twenty years since I seen a rescue of a Fair Maiden in the crystal ball and that was a fireman. Well, what else. If you'll spend the night in the alley just across from this place, here, right after midnight the restaurant will throw out two T-bone steaks, medium-rare, not even touched. Man and his wife have an anniversary fight and storm outa the place without eatin'. What else. You expectin' a horse, maybe?''

Prince Charming said he was not expecting a horse.

'''Fiuzyou, I'd expect a horse. *Also,* there's somethin' in here about a Holiday comin' up in about two days. Oh, boy, that means the Duke of Eyes'll be at it again. That machine goes through Fair Maidens like they was panty hose. That's it.''

''What's it?''

''That's yer fortune. Coupon please. Thank you very much.''

Prince Charming found himself back on the street. It was late enough to seek shelter for the night, and by paying strict attention to what the fortune-teller had told him, he was able to obtain two medium-rare steaks, two baked potatoes, one with butter one with sour cream, and a side of fried zucchini. As he sprawled in the rear doorway of the restaurant, licking his fingers, he thought how true it was that one's pleasures are measured by one's expectations. He could not remember having had a better or more satisfying meal.

Were it not for the plight of the Fair Maiden, he would have been almost content. He still had no idea how to find the colosseum when the terrible day came.

# CHAPTER 16

ON THE DAYS that followed, Marianne would wake each morning to look out the high, barred window at a featureless sky, rather more gray than blue, without clouds, perhaps evenly painted with a high mist through which the sun let down a neutral, colorless light. She would rise wearily, use the toilet, splash tepid water on her face and chest at the stained basin, then retreat to the cot to await breakfast. It would always be the same; bread and tea, both tasteless. During the morning, the voice at the grating would offer intelligence of a kind. Lunch would follow; broth and bread, distinguishable from the previous meal only in that the liquid was served in a bowl rather than a cup. During the afternoon, the voice through the wall would hiss its messages of cheer, and in the evening there would be bread and a kind of mush that seemed to have a good deal of sawdust in it in addition to whatever nutrient it might have contained. Shortly after the evening meal, the light would go out as the shrieks began, and in the scream-wracked darkness she would lie awake, shaking and weeping silently while the puppies huddled around her, offering what comfort they could.

The voice through the wall told her foolproof ways of escaping the Duke of Eyes: running around him clockwise to make him dizzy; putting marbles under his wheels to make him skid; picking up a rock from the arena floor and using it to bash in his sensors. Hearing this merely increased Marianne's sense of hopelessness. Each tidbit was so obviously constructed to make her try desperate maneuvers in the arena, to increase her spectator value.

The voice from the hallway, however, gave her intelligence about her champion. How he tried to buy new clothing but could not pay for it in coin of the realm. How his sword has rusted into its sheath so it could not be drawn out. How he had attempted to meet with Marianne prior to the day of the trial only to have his request denied by the magistrates. About his piteous state of dishevelment and pathetic lack of armor. About his maplessness and homelessness and probable inability even to find the colosseum on the holiday. At each such recitation, the sluggish, nameless entity within Marianne stirred, each time more restively, as though about to awake. It was like being in a small boat, she thought, above the heaving of some great waterbeast that lifted and sagged the surface in dizzying waves so that her whole world tilted from the rising pressure of the monstrous thing beneath. Each time, Marianne retched, staggered, and then came to herself, unchanged yet newly terrified that the next time whatever it was would come up, breach the surface, and terrify her by letting her look into its face. When that happened . . . when that happened, she assured herself, she could not possibly survive it.

"It's six of one and half a dozen of the other," she wept hysterically into the flat mattress. "Whether I die of this heaving inside me or die at the hands or feet or whatever of the Duke of Eyes. Whichever comes first, I suppose." Beneath the cot a moist nose and tongue touched her dangling hand, as though in comfort, and she dug her fingers into the loose skin of a pup. They were still there, still coming and going, present in twos and threes, always absent when anyone might be looking. If she could only find their route of entry. If she could only find one of her own.

So, each day. She lost count of them. There were ten or a dozen, all alike. Then the morning came on which the sky was a clear, empyrean blue, on which a fresh wind enlivened the cells with stomach-heaving smells of food and smoke, and on which some nearby loudspeaker broke the morning quiet with the blared announcement, "The Queen is pleased to announce a HOLIDAY. All citizens are reminded of the obligation to visit a church or temple of your choice."

Her cell door swung wide. A heavy-bellied guardsman told her to come along to church services, and she found herself in the company of some fifty or sixty other inmates, all with the same lost and shattered expression on their faces, being herded into a vaulted room crowded with images and symbols and hazed with rising veils of ceremonial smoke.

The service was conducted interminably in a language foreign to all those present. They bore it patiently as it wound its way through procession and recession, prophon and antiphon, prolapse and relapse, to its long delayed close. When they left the vault, blinking at the sudden access of light, they were given chunks of dried cake to eat and herded onto a waiting bus. Only when the bus approached the gates of the colosseum—which Marianne seemed to remember having seen before, whether personally or on TV she could not say—did she realize that this was the day of her trial. She tried to scream, but her mouth was full of dried cake, and she succeeded only in spraying gummy crumbs over an old woman sitting next to her and receiving an indignant glance and muttered curses in return.

She did not see where they took the others. They dragged her down a flight of worn stone stairs into the bowels of the place, into a kind of cell with two barred doors, one opening from the echoing corridor and the other into the arena itself. Through this grated opening she could hear and see the crowds streaming into the towering stands, could observe the velvet-draped grandeur of the royal box. This baroque edifice was garlanded with golden rope. Slender pillars reached from it to a gilded baldachin over the carved throne. Marianne clutched the bars and stared at it as though hypnotized, waiting for the moment when that dark woman would arrive.

The Duke of Eyes entered first.

From behind a mighty timbered door, a stupendous clatter overrode the crowd noises, a cacaphonous thunder that shocked the muttering multitude into silence. As they watched, nudging one another, the vast door rose on creaking ropes and through it came the Duke himself.

Treads as high as Marianne's head moved inexorably with a metallic clanging. Between and above them towered a cylindrical housing with swinging tentacles on either side. Above that projected the top of a glass-fronted coffin with something barely discernible in it, a form that might have been human.

In one tentacle it carried a bludgeon; in another a flame thrower; in another a sword; in the last a lash made up of many little chains. The crowd roared. The Queen moved into the royal box and took her seat. Across from Marianne a barred door opened and a man was thrust out into the arena, half naked, bare-handed. He stared at the creature before him with horror and dismay.

Marianne watched as long as she could. For a time the man was agile enough to escape injury. After the Duke broke one of his legs with the bludgeon, however, the contest was less amusing and the crowd began to complain, querulously, like a hive of angry bees. The Queen watched all this with no change of expression. As Marianne turned away, her stomach heaving and the sound of the man's screams echoing in her ears, a voice spoke from behind her.

"Maiden? Marianne?"

He stood in the doorway. Someone had opened the grating to let him through. The tattered finery that hung upon him was caked with alley dirt and thrown ordure. His trousers were mere scraps, clinging to his thighs more out of habit than from any sensible continuity of fabric. His feet were wrapped in scraps of velvet rag, and his shirt was a filthy fiction. She stared, unable to believe him, even while knowing who it must be.

"I could not obtain a map," he said with some dignity. "So I merely followed the crowds. I'm sorry I'm so late."

"You're my champion?" she asked, breaking into hysterical giggles. "The man who will fight for me? Prince Charming?"

Something in his face stilled her helpless merriment. It was stern, hard, aching and yet determined. He crossed the room and stared through the window she had just left.

"So," he said. "That's what Madame has waiting for us."

"You can't fight it," she told him. "No one can."

Across the cell a yellow puppy slid between two stones to sit panting on the floor.

"If we can't fight it, we have to escape it," he told her. "You hear me, Fair Lady!"

The thing inside Marianne heaved. She retched with motion sickness as her interior landscape trembled.

"A nice trick that would be," she said with a sick, feeble giggle, tears running down her face. "Maybe it will kill us quickly."

"Not on your life it won't," he said. "Maiden! Listen to me. We have to find a way out!"

"If we just lie down. Put our heads down. Don't move, no matter how much it hurts us. . . ."

He came to her, the strength of him pouring before him like a palpable cloud. He took her in his arms as though it were a ritual and pressed his lips to hers. She could not move, could not breathe. She wanted to thrust him away but more than that to lose herself in that embrace and never come out of it. The thing inside her heaved again, and again, higher and higher, breaking upward through all the strata that had overlaid it, all the time, the endless time . . .

"My Prince!" cried *Marianne,* who had been sleeping for about ten years.

"Who are you?" cried Marianne at once and in the same voice. Something besides herself occupied her mind.

"Beloved," Prince Charming cried, exultantly. "Sleeping Beauty. My own!"

"Where?" *Marianne* asked, staring around herself at the stone walls, cocking her head at the screams of the crowd. "Where are we?"

"We are ensorceled, enchanted, girded about with foul machination," he said. "In about five minutes, they'll kill us—you and me. There should be some way to escape. All ensorcelments have escape hatches. . . ."

Behind them, a blue dog slipped into the cell, closely followed by a silver one.

"What's going on?" begged Marianne. "What's happening?"

"Shh, shh," said *Marianne*. "Be still. Let me see what you know." There was another of those seasick heavings, and Marianne felt her body move, without her volition, to the barred gate. "Oh, Gods of Creation, what monster is that?"

"A very horrid one," he answered. "A crippled thing in both mind and body, given the wherewithal to accomplish its foul purposes despite its limitations."

"We can't fight him."

"Not conceivably."

"We must find a way out."

A black puppy slipped into the room, a red one close behind him, and with a rending shudder, the hoof and leg of a horse reached through just behind them.

"Oh, most elevated and supreme Prince, most lovely Lady, guidance!" whinnied a pathetic voice. "I am lost among the stones, tracking these wee doglings, and cannot find my way."

"Who is that?" The Prince turned toward the wall. "Who calls my name?"

"Your faithful steed, left behind in the void, oh, Prince. Shout again, and I will follow the sound of your voice."

The red dog disappeared into the stone, and the other front leg of the horse emerged, along with its nose. The black dog leapt up, seized the bridle, and tugged the horse forward. It nodded its head and neighed gratefully as the last of its tail came through the stone, then turned confidentially to Marianne. "Lovely Lady, though I would walk through hell for the privilege of your company, I had not thought to make such a trip as that." He turned his massive head as though to look at himself. He was a ponderous gray Shire horse, feather-footed and muscular, his back a veritable field on which a high saddle sat like a minaret, garlanded about with weapons.

"My steed?" asked the Prince, uncertainly. "The fortune-teller did tell me to expect a horse."

"Obviously," said the horse. "What good is a Prince Charming without his faithful horse?"

The five dogs sat down in a row and regarded Marianne with a mixture of skepticism and concern. They had grown considerably since she had seen them last.

"Are you really my doggies?" she asked at last, the words

scarcely out of her mouth before someone else inside her used her mouth to ask quite another question.

"Haven't we met before?"

Black Dog panted, nodding. "Elsewhere, *Marianne*. And in another time."

Red Dog nodded assent. "An evil place, this. We find ourselves very limited in what we can do to assist you."

"Would your limitations extend to getting us out of here?" Prince Charming asked, his eyes fixed on the royal box where the Queen seemed about to make an announcement.

"There is an available nexus, yes," said Black Dog. "One. We know the momeg who holds a locus upon it, one Gojam, and he would be happy to let us through. His locus is, however, in an unfortunate juxtaposition relative to certain other material manifestations."

"I don't understand." The Prince wrinkled his brow and rubbed his forehead while Marianne engaged in an internal colloquy between herselves. "You propose a way out? But say it is in an unfortunate place?"

"The spatial location to which we refer is out in the arena. Right in the middle. Under him," said the momeg, pointing with one paw at the Duke of Eyes. "Immediately under him. If you can get us all out there in the middle, Prince, I think we may be able to do something. . . ."

In the arena the Duke of Eyes rumbled to and fro over the bloodstained patch of sand that had been his earlier opponent. Though he moved backward and forward and from side to side, he stayed generally in the center of the area in order to permit the audience the best possible unobstructed view. The Duke seemed to enjoy the sound of his treads, a rhythmic clumpety-wump-de-clangedy-wham which filled the blind-walled chasm with thundering echoes. This clattering stopped briefly as the Queen rose to her feet. Her voice filled the stadium, seeming to need no artificial amplification.

"Loyal Citizens," she cried. "For your delectation, we will now have a trial by combat. Just Marianne, guilty of receiving goods stolen from the palace—the evidence is there, before you," she made two dramatic gestures, first toward a litter being carried around the arena on which the five gemmed crowns rested, then toward the barred gate. "Represented by her champion, Prince Charming!"

The grating flew upward and two guardsmen entered to escort the Prince into the arena. He, however, had already leapt upon his horse and, heaving Marianne up behind him, he shouted a battle cry and thundered into the fray. The momegs, after only a moment's hesitation, pattered after him.

"What are we going to do?" the horse asked in an interested tone. "Do you have anything specific in mind?"

"Get him over to one edge," gritted the Prince. "Away from the middle. Then get ourselves and the dogs into the middle."

"An excellent plan, though somewhat easier said than done," murmured the horse, sidestepping in a set of immaculately executed dressage steps to avoid a tentacle thrust forward by the Duke of Eyes. Momentarily, they were out of the Duke's vision and the crowd cheered.

"Seven to two on the Duke," cried a hawker. "Seven to two on the Duke."

"Ooooh, Marianne," squealed a clutch of colosseum groupies. "Ooooh, Prince Charming." They tossed circlets of flowers which fell around the Prince's head and over the horse's ears, blinding them both. "Ooooh, Hooray for the Duke."

One set of tracks thundered forward, the other back, as the Duke of Eyes rotated to keep them in view. From his central position, it was obvious that the tentacles could reach almost to the arena walls. "Damn little maneuvering room, if you've noticed," the horse whinnied, shaking a flower circlet into his mouth and mumbling around a crisp mouthful of carnations. "Shouldn't you be doing something with that battle axe or that shield or something?"

"Oh, of course," said the Prince, startled. He seized the battle axe and got the shield over one arm just in time to block a sword-bearing tentacle that the Duke lashed at them from behind his left shoulder. The Duke snarled, a metallic growl, twisting his flame-thrower-tentacle toward them. Before it could be brought to bear, both the Black and the Foo Dogs scampered wildly across the arena before the machine, leapt onto the right-hand tread and, running the great treadmill madly on three legs, raised their left hind legs to pee industriously into the gears and linkages. Meantime, the faithful horse had raised himself on his hind legs into a wide, hopping turn that let him pound away in the opposite direction before the flame thrower could be readied for use.

"Got to get him out of the middle," panted Prince Charming. "Got to give him some bait!"

"Me," breathed Marianne. "Me?"

"Me, I'd rather thought," he replied. "I'll slide off. You get forward in the saddle here and hang on. When the thing comes after me, if it does, get behind him in the middle out there with the dogs. Got that?"

"But what about you?" *Marianne* wailed. "What about you!"

"I'll have to run for it," he said grimly, sliding off the wall side of the horse, shield at the ready and battle axe in hand.

Horse and Marianne circled counterclockwise. The Duke of Eyes stopped rotating and concentrated on Prince Charming, now huddled under his shield at the arena wall as though in a state of paralysis. The crowd was on its feet cheering, throwing popcorn, and releasing clouds of brightly colored balloons. The Queen was smiling widely, in very good temper, and now nodded magnanimously, signalling her champion to close in for the kill.

"Twelve to one on the Duke," the hawker cried. "Get yer bets down. Twelve to one on the Duke."

Whatever victims the Duke had met in the past, he was not accustomed to meeting armed opponents. He lashed out clumsily with the flame thrower in an attempt to knock the shield to one side. The Prince jumped high, thrust down with the shield to catch the tentacle beneath it, then cut it through with a mighty swing of the axe while the crowd cheered.

The Queen frowned.

The cheering stopped as though cut off by a knife. The crowd murmured disapprobation. "Foul," several sycophantic voices called. "Foul."

"Five to one on the Duke," the hawker cried again. "Five to one on the Duke."

The Prince retreated behind his shield once more and circled. The Duke's remaining weapons could not be used at a distance.

The mighty treads began to revolve, shrieking as they did so. That same flowering rust that had bloomed on everything metal in the city now bloomed on the gears that moved the great treads. Swiveling and lurching, the Duke scrabbled toward the Prince crabwise, each movement accompanied by an ear-shattering shriek of corroding metal.

Behind the Duke, the horse and Marianne moved on tiptoe toward the center of the arena, dogs at either side.

Prince Charming stuck his head up from behind the shield to stick out his tongue at the Duke. "The Queen is a coprophagist," he cried in a stentorian voice. "She's got steatopygia and her eyes are crossed!"

The Queen scowled. The crowd sat down, huddling in their thousands, making no sound.

"Nyaa, nyaa, nyaa," cried the Prince. "Old metal guts, afraid to fight."

The Queen snarled and gestured: Forward!

The Duke of Eyes extended all remaining tentacles and lunged, only to find himself skidding wildly to the right because of the rust that had largely immobilized one tread.

From behind the mechanical monster, the Black Dog barked wildly. "Now, Prince. Here, Prince, here Prince, here!"

Prince Charming dropped shield and axe and ran for his life. Behind the Duke of Eyes the horse began to occult, winking in and out of existence, each time longer between reappearances. The momegs, too, began to wink. The crowd rose to its feet, screaming. The Queen made an imperious gesture, and the great machine lifted and turned, ponderously creaking and screaming, even as Prince Charming threw himself across the last few feet to the center of the arena and caught the momentarily visible horse around one rear leg.

Then they were gone.

With a scream of rage, the Queen turned and stormed out of the arena. With a clatter of treads, the Duke of Eyes wobbled through the great, timbered door. Later the people of whatever-city-it-was commented upon the strange lights that moved all night in the high, private wing of the palace.

# CHAPTER 17

SLICK AS A frog's back, clay-gray, the flats stretched from under the wagon wheels in all directions to the veiled horizon. Water covered most of it, a mere sheen of moisture licking at mud edges, flattening the hollows, leaving only a narrowly wandering track above the waterline to glimmer like light on wet silk, an uncertain highway from somewhere to anywhere. Tracks came spinning endlessly off the wheels and meandered across the flats until they vanished into misty distance, the net result of all peregrinations yielding no particular direction. Four dogs, red and blue, gray and yellow, bent to the traces, following the black lead dog as he tracked the ridge to leave their paw, wheel and hoof prints in the firmly silted sand. It was forever from where they were to where the tracks vanished in mist. An equivalent featureless distance lay on every hand.

At times the drier ground split into two or three branches, making the lead dog whine with frustration until the momeg, Gojam, flicked the whip in one direction or another to indicate the chosen route. Nothing differentiated the choices. There was always as much water on one hand as on the other; there was always an equivalency of mud, a sufficiency of glimmer, shine, vapor, colorlessness, sourceless, shadowless light.

"A dull world," said Gojam to no one in particular, "yet one I have always favored."

"These are tidal flats, aren't they?" asked Prince Charming.

"So I have always believed," Gojam replied with a polite smile that showed his pointed teeth and crinkled several of his red little eyes.

"Then the tide ought to—come in, oughtn't it? At some time?"

"So I would suppose. Though I have never seen it do so."

"You come here often?"

"When it seems appropriate."

"May one ask," whinnied the horse from his position at the rear of the wagon, "what made it seem appropriate on this occasion?"

"Well," Gojam mused for a moment, his dewlaps quivering and his long, pendant ears swaying to and fro with the power of his concentration. "Firstly, it isn't inimical. I mean, you can all breathe here, and the temperature isn't unbearable. Secondly, it's a placid sort of place. Very little happens. At least, very little has happened when I've been here in the past. I thought that would give you all time to collect yourselves, as it were. . . ."

"Very kind of you," murmured Marianne, wondering if her tenant, *Marianne*, would interrupt her in mid-speech. "I, for one, could stand a little collecting."

"And, thirdly," the momeg continued, "I doubt that half a dozen momegs in the universe know about this place. Which means that though the dark woman, the Queen, Madame Delubovoska, will probably track you here eventually, it isn't likely to be a place she'll look for you right away."

"Madame Delubovoska," mused the Prince. "That was the woman who was attempting to kill us, wasn't it?"

"I believe so," offered Gojam. "Switching nexi is a strain, and you may have forgotten. Let me take the liberty of reminding you. You were engaged in battle with a large, mechanical monster. Does that that ring a bell? Ah, good. Your momeg friends approached me for a means of escape? Ah, you do recall."

"I remember *that*," said the Prince. "I went there to rescue a Fair Maiden—my own true love," he cast Marianne a melting glance, "But how I got there I really can't recollect."

The lead dog stopped, abruptly, making the other four dogs pile up in the traces with muttered growls. "Something," the Black Dog said. "Out there on the mud."

They stared in the direction the dog's muzzle pointed, seeing nothing at first, then a tiny interruption in nothing, and finally, protruding above the water, two miniscule pimples that had attracted the dog's attention. The pimples blinked and disappeared, only to appear again, slightly to the right of their previous location.

"Eyes," said Marianne. "Something with eyes."

The eyes regarded them balefully from the level of the water's surface before disappearing again. They might have been something quite small, close up, or something quite large, far away.

"I had no idea anything lived here," Gojam remarked, scratching at a left ear with one pair of arms while twitching the reins with another. "Of course, I haven't come here that frequently."

"About the tide," said the Prince, moodily attempting to pull two scraps of trouser together to cover an expanse of muscular thigh. "Reason would indicate it must come in at some time or other."

"I've always thought reason sadly overrated," remarked Gojam. "There are momegs who pay a lot of attention to it, just as there are some who disbelieve in it entirely. I tend to the middle view. Use it when it's helpful and ignore it when it isn't."

"I merely meant, it would be unpleasant for us if the tide came in while we were out here." The Prince sighed, turned to Marianne, gave her a long, burning look and touched her hand. *Marianne* stroked his in response, her eyes misty. The hand twitched and drew away as Marianne looked down and saw what it was doing.

"You say 'out here' as though there were some 'in there' which might be selected instead," Gojam commented, uncrossing his third and fourth legs and stretching them over the dashboard of the wagon. "So far as I am aware, 'out here' is all there is."

"Wrong," said the horse. "It may be all you've seen, magnificent sir. All you have become aware of in your peregrinations. All you have intuited or assumed or inferred from the lack of structure around us. Not all, however, that there is. I suggest you gaze toward the horizon, slightly to the left of our present line of travel."

"I see it," said the Red Dog after a time. "A tower."

"Towers," corrected Blue Dog. "Misty, but still quite real."

"I wouldn't have said real," murmured Gojam. "Evident, perhaps. Or perceivable. Not necessarily real."

"A nice philosophical point," commented the Prince, perking up a little. "Could we direct our travel in the direction of those possibly spiritual and/or ephemeral structures?"

Gojam sighed, flicked the whip, and directed Black Dog slightly to the left at the next branch.

"Eyes," said Marianne again, pointing toward the water. This time there were several pairs of lidded hemispheres blinking at them from the fluctuating surface.

"They seem interested in our progress but not hostile," Gojam remarked. "In keeping with the placidity I have always found here."

"Wherever here is," neighed the horse rudely, mostly to himself.

"How did you and the—the other momegs become acquainted?" Marianne asked hastily, giving the horse's nose an admonitory tap of her fingers.

"Become acquainted?" Gojam stared at her with one set of eyes, rapidly blinking the other to convey confusion. "I am not aware that we are acquainted."

"I only thought—you were kind enough to let them exit through your . . . your locus."

"Through a nexus of which my locus was a part, most accurately. It's impossible to exit through a locus. A locus doesn't go anywhere. It merely is. Interminably and dully in most cases. Which is not responsive to your inquiry. Well, I would have done as much for any entity. Known or unknown. Recognizable or strange. Dynamic or static. Your friends approached me politely and I responded in kind. What kind of a universe would it be if we could not do small kindnesses for one another?''

"I see," she murmured. "What indeed."

"Besides," he confessed, compressing one set of lips while sneering with another, "I do detest Madame Delubovoska. She has a nasty habit of summoning up momegs on the spur of the moment, without any concern for the inconvenience it may cause, and then splatting them back again whenever it suits her. If she returns them at all, which I have reason to doubt in some cases. A very *very* close friend of mine, virtually a contiguite, was used twice by Madame and actually burned both times as a dismissal. No lasting damage, of course. We're virtually indestructible, but we do have *feelings*.''

"How awful for him," murmured Marianne, feeling faintly guilty without being able to remember why. "How awful for you. How many—ah, contiguites do you have?"

"Oh, twelve. Depending upon the packing, don't you know. They do insist on shifting it about.''

"Twelve at my locus, too," said the Black Dog. "Of course, it's unstressed space in my neighborhood. Things can get packed a lot tighter than that around singularities, I understand.''

"Indeed," said Gojam, playing idly with the whip. "So I've been told by some momegs who've been there. And a lot looser around discontinuities, if it comes to that—which we all fervently hope it never does." He shuddered delicately. "No matter how dull the locus, it's better than no locus at all." He sighed, moodily. "Are we getting any closer to the whatevers?"

They were getting considerably closer. What had at first appeared to be towers now proved to be lumpish promontories culminating in tall, cylindrical structures that were either unfinished or in a state of ruinous decay.

"Eyes," said Marianne again. This time there were a hundred pairs or more, moving gently along the surface of the water, observing their progress.

"A veritable metropolis, gentlemen and lady," suggested the horse. "An urban center. Who knows what delights and surprises may await us.''

"Whatever it is, it's made out of mud," remarked the Red Dog. "Wet mud."

"Wettish," corrected Black Dog. "If it were really wet, it wouldn't hold shape."

"Not necessarily true," admonished Gojam. "There you go, naughty, naughty, being reasonable again. You have to remember where we are."

"Wherever that may be," nickered the horse, very quietly, to himself.

"Wherever it is, we approach," said the Black Dog, firmly.

As they drew closer, they could see that the structures were indeed made of mud, tiny dab on tiny dab built up in endless layers, like the nest of a cliff swallow or a mud dauber wasp, the accretion of protracted and focused effort, mud on mud on mud, higher and higher, a mighty mound with little jug-shaped dwellings covering it, the round jug necks peering in all directions. At the top of the great mound a slightly smaller mound began, and on top of that one, another still. Extending high above these three great clumps, like a mud-man with a tall hat, a long cylindrical chimney of mud dabs spiralled lumpishly upward into the mists.

"Wettish," remarked the Black Dog with satisfaction. "Damp."

"Hail, great travelers," called a small voice. "Accept the hospitality of the Tower of Petition."

It took them a little time to locate the speaker. It had crawled out of the water onto the track before them and lay there now, propped high on two front flippers with its eyes bulging toward them, the top of its head reaching approximately to Black Dog's knees.

"Hail," said Gojam in a kindly voice. "Very nice of you, I must say."

The speaker flipped itself toward the mud hive, found an upward track among the dwellings and scuttled up this slick and obviously well-traveled incline until it was at their eye level. "I would invite you in, but there seems to be some disparity in size."

"Think nothing of it," said the Prince. "We may have been

trespassing. If so, it was unintentional, and we apologize for any anxiety we may have caused.''

The speaker waved both flippers before its face as though to wave away such an idea. ''We are honored by your presence. Some of us have been following your progress with deep attention. Even now our philosophers are engaged in colloquy to determine which of the Great Questions should be put to you. Who knows? Your arrival may actually put an end to Construction!''

''Construction?'' asked Marianne. ''This construction?'' She gestured upward at the tower. ''It's very impressive. We wouldn't want to . . . interrupt anything.'' Her eyes dropped to the water level where great numbers of the mud creatures were scuttling up into and upon the building. Many of the mud jugs were already occupied, and serious eyes peered at them from every direction.

''It would be a blessing,'' the speaker said in a distracted tone. ''We've been building it with conscript labor for sixty generations, and everyone is tired to death of it. Is there anything I can do to increase your comfort? The water is potable. At least, we drink it. If you'd like some scum, I can have some gathered for you. No? We quite understand. Different creatures, different needs. Though until now we had only postulated the existence of different creatures. And now! To see—how many kinds of you are there? I count at least four, but perhaps there are subtleties of which I am unaware?''

''Three basic shapes,'' said the Prince. ''Four if you distinguish on the basis of size as you seem to be doing. Two basic kinds. Nine entities, each different in some way from the others. I believe there are at least three sexes represented.''

''Oh, you,'' said Gojam, twinkling.

''Remarkable,'' twittered the mud creature. ''Oh, I am incredibly rude. I haven't given you my designation. I am philosopher's assistant Puy.''

''I am Prince Charming,'' said the Prince. ''This is the Fair Maiden Marianne or Sleeping Beauty Marianne, I forget which. That is Gojam. That is a horse, nameless for the moment, though undoubtedly faithful. The dogs are all momentary gods, as is Gojam, designated by color."

"Color?" asked Puy. "I'm sorry, I don't recognize the concept."

"Ah, a measure of the creature's ability to reflect certain wavelengths of light. Unimportant."

"They are Rouge, Delphy, Liquorice, Gold, and Silver," said Marianne, pointing to each in turn.

"Delighted," said Puy, bowing on his flippers. "Utterly delighted. Ah, I believe the council of philosphers is approaching."

Having made this announcement, Puy peered upward from the edge of the slide. Following his gaze, they saw several rather bulbous mud creatures sliding down the mud track from the top of the structure, braking madly at the turns with their flippers, then thrusting themselves onward on the straightaways, much in the manner of skiers negotiating a challenging run. They had reached the bottom of the chimney shape and were now negotiating tortuous turns among the dwellings. They arrived, rather out of breath, bowed to Puy, who bowed in return, and then took their positions before the visitors, still panting.

"Honored guests," their spokesman peeped. "We, the council of philosophers, have determined which of the Great Questions shall be put to you."

"Very flattering, I'm sure," said Gojam. "Is it your expectation we will answer this question or questions?"

The mud creatures stared at them, then at each other, murmuring rapidly.

". . . always thought . . ."

". . . never considered they might not . . ."

". . . could always threaten them . . ."

". . . try persuasion . . ."

"We will be happy to try to answer your questions," said *Marianne* in a firm voice, frowning at Gojam.

"I was only asking," said the momeg in a mild voice. "Not all creatures really want their questions answered, you know."

The rapid exchange among the mud peepers went on.

"Trying to answer just isn't good enough. . . ."

". . . anything that size ought to know. . . ."

". . . had to come from somewhere. . . ."

"We have decided to threaten you," the speaker went on at the conclusion of this conference. "You must answer the questions."

"Or?" asked Prince Charming, curiously.

"Or we'll summon the tide," the creature answered.

"It will wash away your entire building," the Prince remarked, with what Marianne regarded as commendable calm. "Would you really want to do that?"

The conference resumed.

". . . hadn't thought about . . ."

". . . sixty generations by my count. . . ."

". . . all to do over again. . . ."

"Maybe we'll just ask the questions," the speaker said at last, eyes half shut and an expression of pain on its fishlike face.

"Ask away," invited Gojam.

"We've been building this tower for over sixty generations," the speaker peeped. "Trying to get it high enough to see over the mist. You've probably noticed, you can't see very far."

"We had noticed," Marianne said.

"We were trying to answer several of the great questions for ourselves you see. It isn't that we're lazy, or lacking in endeavor. We've really worked very hard at this. It's difficult, you know. The mud won't dry thoroughly. It tends to slide. There've been some really bad accidents. . . ."

"Your question?" asked Gojam.

"We need to know two things. Where are we, and is there anyone out there who can help us?"

Gojam frowned and began to speak, then frowned again. When he did speak, it was very gently. "You're on a world in the dream zone, which I identify as the Mud Flats."

There was a long silence, broken at last by Puy. "That . . . that isn't really helpful to us. I think what the philosophers want an answer to is the second question. Is there anyone out there who can help us?"

Gojam began to shake his head. Prince Charming very firmly took him by the neck and held him still.

"It would help us if you told us why you wanted to know."

"Why . . . we *need* to know," asserted Puy. "There are certain problems we have been unable to solve. We have been unable even to agree on possible solutions. Basic philosophies differ. There is the question of the hatch rate, should it be encouraged or discouraged or should it be a matter of personal choice. There is the question of those among us who prefer not to provide their share of labor. Should they be conscripted against their will, and if not, are the rest of us under any obligation to feed them. There is the question of mechanicals. Some say they are diabolical and against the Will Of Him Who. Others maintain they are quite acceptable. We have come to bites and thrashings over these questions. Blood has been shed. Several of us have suffered quite severe lacerations. If there were someone neutral, someone from outside, who would arbitrate, perhaps give us another point of view. . . ."

Gojam started to speak again, but the Prince held him firmly. "You're saying there is considerable disagreement among you about how to solve your problems?"

The chief philosopher spoke up, nodding vigorously. "Indeed. There is no agreement on how things should be handled. None at all. We need . . ."

"You need someone who will tell you what to do?"

"Well . . ." They scurried together for another hurried colloquy.

". . . Not *tell*, precisely. . . ."

". . . still it wouldn't be a bad idea. . . ."

"I can answer your question," the Prince interrupted them. "Yes, there are many worlds and creatures out there. Your next question will be, how do you reach them? Well, you cannot reach them until you have solved your own problems. And, no, we cannot help you with your problems. It is forbidden for us to do so. Each society must solve its own problems before it goes mixing about with other societies. That's the law. Isn't that right, Gojam?"

Gojam sulked only for a moment. "Perfectly correct, Prince. Exactly what I was going to say."

"In return for this information," Prince Charming continued, inexorably, "We'd like to ask a favor."

"Anything," breathed the philosophers sadly, banging their faces on their flippers, "anything at all."

"We have an enemy. A tall person shaped like one of us," the

Prince indicated Marianne and himself. "A female person, if that concept is meaningful. She has a lot of very dark hair—this stuff. She is thinner than this person. She is as tall as I am. She has very fiery—ah, let me see—very intense-looking eyes. She may ask if you have seen us. She would not hesitate to destroy you if she did not get information to her liking."

"Say no more," breathed Puy. "No more. At the first sight of such a one, we will summon the tide."

"But your extraordinary building," murmured Marianne.

"Thanks be to all the things that are or may be, we can quit building the damned thing," Puy said. "It's been very tiring. You have no idea. It's virtually destroyed our social system. Blessings on you for bringing us the law. Really." He turned and kicked at a bit of mud with his right flipper, watching it with satisfaction as it tumbled into the water and dissolved. All over the structure, mud creatures were ripping off chunks of building material and dropping them to see the splash.

There seemed nothing further to discuss. Gojam flicked his whip. They moved off into the mist.

"Is what you said really the law?" *Marianne* asked.

"It is here," murmured the Prince. "It is now."

When they had followed the wavering track until they could barely see the towers far behind them, Gojam muttered, "Well, enough of this, all right? Where now? Someplace Madame won't even consider looking for you. I have one or two ideas. . . ."

"No," said Prince Charming. "Our encounter with these mud creatures has brought me to confront the true problem we face. We can run from her for a very long time, but it won't solve anything. Just as our mud friends have to solve their own problems, so do we."

Marianne started to say something, then stopped, her tongue checked by that other person who seemed to be sharing her body. That person, in turn, stepped away, as though conscious she had been rude. In their common mind, Marianne could hear the half-humorous, half-hysterical laughter of that other person. "After you, Marianne."

"I was just going to say we have more problems than one." Her voice was stiff and unforgiving, and she glared at the Prince as though it had been his fault, only to feel the glare turn into a wry smile as that other *Marianne* peered through her eyes.

"I know," he said. "I know. There are two of you in there, and I love at least one of you desperately. Since there were no provisions for that emotion in the world we fled from, it is obvious to me that the world from which we fled is not the world in which we belong. Gojam, can you take us through to our own real world?"

The momeg looked disappointed as he quirked his various eyebrows and twitched various pairs of extremities. "Of course. There's a likely nexus only a few steps from here. Though you have various real worlds. You, sir, have one. The woman has one. The other woman I sense to be present has another. The other momegs have their loci . . . well, you take my meaning."

"I do." Prince Charming mused, still attempting to draw the shreds of his clothing together, compulsively, as though he could find refuge behind or within some whole garment. "Our basic problem seems to be Madame Delubovoska. Though I cannot at the moment remember why she is a difficulty for us. Still, it is evident we cannot accomplish anything without dealing with her. Presumably she has a place in the real world. We should, therefore, be returned as near that place as we can be without endangering ourselves. If we have allies anywhere near, then we would like to go to the place our allies dwell."

"I will drop you," Gojam said in his usual kindly voice, "in the vicinity of Alphenlicht."

# CHAPTER 18

"BUT MY DEAR, if you didn't tell the creature precisely where you wanted to be left off, you shouldn't be angry if he just dropped you nearby." Ellat offered Marianne a towel. "Perhaps dung doesn't mean to it what it does to us."

Though Marianne did not remember Ellat, the woman's astonishing familiarity and friendliness did not permit Marianne to react as to a stranger. "A dung pile is a dung pile," Marianne objected. "And I don't for one moment think Gojam didn't know it."

"What was it you said it was? A momentary god? Makr Avehl mentioned momentary gods just before he went after you."

"Gojam, the one with the peculiar sense of humor, went back, wherever they go. We have the other five with us, the dog ones."

"Aghrehond said something about it. I suggested the kennels, but he . . . he didn't think that would do."

"They're not really dogs, you know, Ellat. Not really."

"As for that, Marianne, who are you, really?" The older woman turned Marianne around so she could look into her eyes. "Are you the girl I knew?"

131

"Yes," said *Marianne*.

"No," said Marianne.

It came out as a gargle.

"You're not sure," Ellat offered in a sympathetic tone. "Or maybe you're both."

"An uncomfortable both," *Marianne* said, gritting her teeth. "The thinking part works well, thank you. We each seem to have control of our own thoughts. But sometimes both of us try to use the body at once. I go left, she goes right. I say yes, she says no. We seem to gargle and stagger a lot. Well, you get the idea."

"Not at all pleasant," agreed Ellat. "Couldn't you agree to take turns?"

"It may come to that," Marianne agreed, closing her eyes wearily. "Except that I'm still half convinced this whole thing is a dream. Did Makr Avehl tell you about the world he found me in?"

Ellat shook her head. Actually, he had said a few words, but only a few, and most of those had had to do with Madame Delubovoska.

"I was managing a laundry," Marianne mused.

"The Cave of Light showed him a woman washing clothes," Ellat offered. "I imagine that's how he found you."

"What I can't understand is why? Even in dream there should be some logic. Why a laundry?"

Ellat stirred, a little uncomfortably. "You might discuss that with Therat. . . ."

"Therat?"

"One of the Kavi. She is extremely interested in the power of symbols. I imagine she'll tell you that the laundry was symbolic of something in your life. Some need for cleanliness or being cleansed of something. Some unexpressed wish for redemption, perhaps. Madame summoned you into her world, but your own conscious or subconscious symbolic structure would largely have determined the specific role you would play in that environment. At least, that's my understanding of the way it works."

"A laundry!" Marianne shook her head. "And then there's this business of memory only working one way! When I'm there, I can't remember here. But when I'm here, I can remember there well enough. Not like a dream at all, which is upsetting, because if it's all a dream, which I believe it is, then I ought not to be able to remember it. Unless I'm not awake yet.'' She made a petulant gesture, aware of how ridiculous this sounded. ''Well, let it go. I think the important thing for me now is to find out about air schedules to get home. If it's a dream, I'll dream my flight back. I may have already lost my job, not showing up for so long.''

''How long do you think, my dear?''

''Days. Weeks. Maybe months. No—only weeks, I think.''

''Actually, less than one day.''

''You're joking?''

''Not at all. It was only last night that we awoke, Makr Avehl and I, knowing something had happened to you. It is only a few hours since Aghrehond went after Makr Avehl. Time does not move in the false worlds as it moves here. Madame can do a year's worth of damage in the false worlds in what passes for moments here in our world. In the dream worlds, one can live many lives in one lifetime or one can effectively experience an eternity of discomfort or horror.''

Both Mariannes took a moment to absorb this. ''Well, little time or a lot, I've still got to get back to work,'' said the younger one. She rose with a bit of bustle, wanting to do something decisive, tired of being done to and with.

''Marianne,'' said Makr Avehl from the doorway where, clad only in clean trousers, he stood vigorously toweling his head. ''Don't be silly. You can't.'' His voice was fond, loving, concerned.

''I most certainly can,'' she turned, eyes blazing, furious at his assumption of authority over her.

His lips clamped tight in disappointment and anger. ''Then you'll most certainly end up back in some laundry, or some library, or some dungeon once again! Madame is not going to give up. Can't you get that through your head?'' He threw the towel on the floor and stamped on it with his bare feet as he left the room, shouting for someone to get him a shirt.

''He doesn't like me,'' said Marianne, slightly discomfitted. ''He really doesn't.''

"It isn't that," Ellat murmured. "But you do rather stand between him and someone he loves very dearly."

"Her," snarled Marianne. "I know." She waited grimly for *Marianne* to assert herself, but there was only a silent, somehow satisfied watchfulness inside.

"True, but it isn't only that. He feels responsible for you. You *both,* I should say. The situation must be resolved, and he's quite right. If you go back home, you'll only end up ensorceled once again."

"If the damned woman wants to kill me, why doesn't she just do it and get it over with? Why all this folderol, this magic this and that. I really don't understand it. Don't believe it. Don't like it."

"Well, my dear, none of us do. As to why she doesn't just hire some thug to murder you—well, the reason is fairly obvious I should think. She doesn't really want you dead. She wants you in a state of subservience. She needs something from you. You really should enquire about your parents' estate, Marianne. If Tabiti is seeking to enslave you, it must be because you have or will have some authority she wants."

"Well, I already have inquired about the estate," Marianne confessed, a little shamefacedly. "When Makr Avehl visited our home, he said something about it which piqued my curiosity, so I asked Mama. Evidently my independence has impressed Papa sufficiently that he has named me as the executor, for everything. I had always assumed there would be a number of trustees—and there will be if anything happens to me—but if anything happens to Mama and Papa and I'm alive and well, I'll be the only one."

"Well then, you have the explanation so don't be foolish," said Makr Avehl from the door. He had managed to get himself almost fully dressed, and was now tucking in an unbuttoned shirt that displayed a generous extent of muscular and smooth-skinned chest. "It's obvious what Tabiti wants—just what she's wanted all along: control of the Zahmani estates. She enslaves you, then does away with your parents, and she's what you Americans would call home free."

Marianne withdrew her eyes from Makr Avehl's naked chest, surprised to find that simple action very difficult. "Ah—um, I

did think she was going to kill me, though, there in the arena."
The sight of his body was doing strange things to her breathing.

"I think not. The threat to you was a ploy designed to get me into the act," Makr Avehl said, buttoning his shirt. "Since I represent a challenge to her plans, naturally, she wants me out of the way entirely."

"If she had killed you there, would you be . . . that is, would it have . . ."

"Would it have killed me here and now? Oh, very much so. Because everything that makes me me was there. All that was left here was a kind of anchor."

"And yet when we're . . . there, we don't remember . . . here."

"No, because if we did, we couldn't be fully involved in the dream world. Our memories of home would keep us from interacting with where we are and what we're doing. You couldn't really have been concerned about that laundry if you'd remembered home, could you? Could I have believed in myself as Prince Charming if I had remembered who I was?"

"Does Madame remember who she is when she's there?"

Makr Avehl looked puzzled. "You know, I haven't the least idea. It wouldn't surprise me. In fact, that could be part of the secret of her power, an ability to take her memory intact into the false worlds. It would be quite a trick, wouldn't it, Ellat?"

"It would indeed," she said with a harsh twist to her lips. "Though I hate to think what she must have done to gain that ability. Not something I think we want to try for, Makr Avehl."

"No fear, Sister."

"May I enter, most exalted one?" Aghrehond stood at the door, his hair still wet from the thorough washing he had given it. Of them all, Aghrehond had been most completely buried in the dung pile. "May I greet our guest in my own inimitable person? May I say hello and how-de-do and welcome to Alphenlicht?"

Ellat beckoned him. "Don't be an ass, Hondi. Come in."

"But I am an ass, Lady. Or was. First cousin to one. Did I make an excellent horse, Marianne? Was I splendid?"

"Perfectly splendid, Aghrehond," she choked, fighting her internal twin for possession of her voice.

"I liked you better as the grassy dog," said *Marianne*, taking over. "I liked you as Cani Grassi, Aghrehond. Fighting the Manticore."

Makr Avehl stepped forward to embrace her, holding her very tightly only for a moment, then stepping back as she started to writhe away from him.

"I wish you wouldn't do that," said Marianne, not entirely convincingly. She found herself panting.

"It was the other one I embraced," he whispered. "Don't take it personally."

She, however, was taking it very personally, since every inch of her body yearned toward him. Her limbs felt loosened, somehow separated from her, as though they were floating. Hot, sweet liquid was running through her veins, and there was a tingle in her breasts. She breathed as though she had been running. She sat down abruptly, sending a confused, hostile thought toward her tenant.

*"Damn it, do you have to melt like that?"*

*"I love him, silly girl. What do you want me to do? Simply ignore how I feel?"*

*"I want you to go back where you came from."*

*"I am where I came from. Precisely."*

*"Then go wherever you went when I was twelve."*

*"Not on your life. I tried that, and all it did was almost get us both killed."*

*"What brought you back, anyhow?*

*"You know very well!"* Marianne felt the internal blush.

*"Oh, the Sleeping Princess was awakened by Prince Charming's kiss? Isn't that a dreadful cliché?"*

"Marianne!" Ellat was shaking her. "Stop that. Your eyes are crossed and you're making disgusting noises. If you have to argue with yourself, go out in the garden and do it out loud." She pushed the embarrassed girl out the door and made a gesture at the two men who had been watching, openmouthed. "And as for you two, go away. Makr Avehl, I'm ashamed of you. You're not helping, not at all."

"What do you want me to do, Ellat?" he echoed *Marianne's* silent question. "Pretend she isn't here?"

"You could try that. For a time. While we try or she tries or they try to sort it out."

He gave her a surly look, but did not argue with that particular point. "I've reached a decision, Ellat."

"I thought you might have," she replied mildly, folding the towel he had dropped on the floor. "Since you wouldn't have come back to Alphenlicht, otherwise."

"We're going to have to confront Madame."

"I assumed that, also."

"Sometimes I despair, Ellat. Will I ever be able to surprise you?"

"Yes. If you'd listen to me, ever, it would surprise me enormously. I told you years ago we would have to deal with Tabiti, forthrightly and personally. You, on the other hand, preferred diplomatic maneuver and, more recently, this dream-world pursuit."

"Not my choice!"

"True. However, in my opinion, the best time to have struck at Tabiti would have been immediately on your return from—what shall I say?—episode one. Before you went searching for *Marianne* again. While Tabiti was still confused."

"You overlook one thing," he replied in a dry voice. "If she was confused, which I'm not at all certain of, I was even more so."

"Yes. Well. That's as may be, and nothing was done at the time, so it's fruitless to speak of it. What do you plan now?"

"I plan a visit to the Cave of Light, Ellat. With Marianne. Tabiti gets her power from somewhere. . . ."

"I thought her power had always been attributed to shamanistic influences."

"That's only a label. Yes, I have no doubt she was taught whatever she knows by the black shamans, but what did they teach her? Where does she draw her force from?"

"And if you find out?"

"We must find a way to cut it off. Marianne will never be safe until we do—the world may not be safe until we do."

"You're aware that there is a great deal of risk in such an endeavor."

"So far as I can see, there's more risk in doing nothing. It's a case of being damned if we do and damned if we don't."

Ellat said nothing to this, choosing instead to cling tightly to a serenity of spirit that had cost her a good deal to achieve. He would do it. She could not in good conscience advise otherwise. She would do what she had done so often in the past.

Wait and hope.

# CHAPTER 19

THERAT RECOMMENDED AN afternoon reading from the Cave of Light, then spent the morning hours with Marianne, telling her of the history of the Cave. "I can't expect you to believe in it totally," she smiled, her lips belying her eyes which burned into Marianne's own with a fervid glow. "We do expect that you not come into the Cave as a skeptic. Just be open to whatever happens."

"Do I need to do anything? Learn any chants or responses or anything?"

"Nothing at all. We'll do the reciting. You will need to stand in darkness for a few moments, which makes some people rather dizzy. I'll be next to you and you can hold on to me if you like."

"Do I get to see the—symbols or whatever they are?"

"Certainly. All those present are requested to verify whatever message the Cave seems to be offering."

"What do I wear?"

"Whatever you like. Ellat will give you a robe to cover whatever you're wearing, but that's tradition, not ritual. I've recommended about two o'clock, if that's all right with you."

"I don't know why not," said Marianne. She had been waiting all morning for *Marianne* to interrupt her or supersede her in some action, but nothing of the kind had happened. Still, the sense of being occupied was very strong. *Marianne* had not gone away.

When they arrived at the Cave that afternoon—Ellat, Aghrehond, Makr Avehl and Marianne—Therat, along with Nalavi and Cyram, met them at the entrance cavern and escorted them down the winding, sandy-floored tunnel by the light of flaring lanterns. Every wall, every pillar, every square inch of exposed stone was decorated with symbols; words, phrases, or numbers; some superimposed upon others; some ancient, some newly chiseled or painted on the stone.

They placed their lanterns upon the central altar. Words were chanted that Marianne did not recognize. She knew what they meant, however. In the ancient language of the Magi, the question that the Cave was to answer had been asked. What was the source of Madame's power?

She felt Therat take her arm as the lanterns were turned off. They stood in darkness. Above them the great, perforated bulk of the mountain rested, spongy with micalined worm holes, through which the light from the outer world was reflected in and down, faint glimmerings, no more than the smallest candle glow, falling through all that weight of rock and earth into the cavern below. Light, reflected from leaf or stream or animal or stone. Never twice the same.

"I see light," whispered Marianne.

"The light rests on an hourglass," said Therat.

"A sundial," said Nalavi.

"A clock," said Cyram, all three of them at once, looking in three different directions. Then they were in darkness once more, unrelieved and absolute. After a moment, Therat sighed and struck a light. "Well, Makr Avehl?"

"Time," he said. "The source of her power is time."

"What's the matter, Makr Avehl?" asked *Marianne*. "You don't sound hopeful."

"Time?" he replied. "How does one get at it? What does one do with it? How has she gained access to it?"

"The momentary gods," *Marianne* replied. "They'd know.

They give time its reality, or so they say. No, that's not quite it. They give space its reality, and that gives time its reality.''

Therat stared at her in the glare of the lantern light. "You have spoken with momentary gods?" Therat asked.

"There are five of them with us," Marianne began.

"I summoned them," said *Marianne*. "It's something I learned to do from . . . from Madame, I think. I was in this place, a library, I seem to remember, and she did this thing. Summoned something terrible. All the world was full of snakes, I remember that. And she had this Manticore. She summoned it up, too, from time to time. And she used . . . used the momentary gods to transport people into her worlds, I remember that. She would reach up and twist the tail of a momentary god, and it would establish a nexus and let someone through. Oh, I do remember that.''

"And you learned to do this by merely observing her?''

*Marianne* shook her head, confused. "I'm not sure that's exactly it. Let's say I absorbed enough to do it once, once only, without knowing what I was really doing and without any idea how to undo it.''

"Shamanism," said Therat in a flat, dismissive tone. "Trifling with the structure of the universe. Foolish! Dangerous!''

"Dangerous, yes, but we'll have to deal with it somehow," mused Makr Avehl.

"I still think we ought to talk to the momentary gods," advised *Marianne,* turning toward the entrance of the Cave. "They may tell us something of value.''

Therat came with them to the Residence, where *Marianne* called the momegs. Black Dog came in answer to her call, but he was most unwilling to talk. He arrived. He listened briefly, then vanished. Marianne called him again, he returned to lie on the floor, head on paws, scowling at them all.

"Come on," *Marianne* said. "You know something. You told me the momegs give time its reality, or something like that.''

"It's true," he mumbled. "Each of us holds a chunk. Our birthright, so to speak.''

"How big a chunk?" asked Makr Avehl.

"You don't understand. It's not like that. Not bigness or longness."

"Well tell me, what is it then?"

"What it is, is duration. Or very rarely beginningness."

Makr Avehl was relentless. "Explain that."

Black Dog whined, pawed his nose, gnawed at some imaginary itch on his hind leg, then said, "Something happens. Then after that, something else happens. Let's say, a light wave comes to my locus. It has duration there, a chunk of it, the only size there is, then it has to go somewhere, so it goes to my contiguite. Anyhow, my contiguite has a chunk of duration, too. *After* something happens somewhere else, something happens with him. Usually it's light. Sometimes it's quarks. We do a lot of durations and aftering with quarks."

"What about beforeness," asked Marianne, puzzled. "Don't any of you have that?"

"There's no such thing," Black Dog barked, almost howling, putting his front paws over his ears. "That's heresy. We give time its reality by duration and afterness. Everything happens after something else. Nothing happens before something else. It can't! That's just a human heresy, that's all."

"Why are you so upset?" asked Makr Avehl. "You're saying time is quantized, aren't you? I don't see why it shouldn't be. Does this have anything to do with where Madame gets her power?"

"She twists things," sulked the Black Dog.

"She's evil," said the Foo Dog, erupting into the room from behind a chair. "She'll end up destroying the universe, or at least this piece of it."

"Because?"

"Because she keeps beforing things. She takes momegs and bends them double, so that things don't go on to after, they twist around and go back before. That's how *she,*" the momeg indicated Marianne, "went back in her own time that way. She learned it from Madame and she borrowed Madame's power to do it. Not that we blame her. She didn't know what she was doing. . . ."

"I really didn't," said *Marianne,* aghast. "Do you mean when I did that, I actually destroyed something?"

"A momeg is all. One of us. Not one any of us liked very much. He was from a locus way out at the edge of things. Madame keeps a stock of rural momegs around. She thinks as long as she just nibbles away at the edges of things, it won't really affect anything. She's wrong, of course. Everyone with any sense knows that the edges of things are really the middle. There have already been disruptions." The Foo Dog brooded. "I suppose we should have told you this be . . . uh, at some prior eventuality."

"It would have been helpful," said Makr Avehl. "I'm not sure I understand it yet. Let's see if I do. The black shamans taught Madame how to evoke momegs. They taught her how to twist momegs in half—is that right?—so that things go backwards or make loops in time instead of going forward?"

"Taught her how, or gave her some device to do it with, I'm not sure which. Anyhow, she does it, and that makes holes in time where she can stick her false worlds," the Foo Dog nodded. "And it allows her to fool around with people in very unpleasant ways. And it's all wrong, of course. Nobody ought to do it, ever. Up until recently, it was only the black shamans who talked about it, but more recently there was some respected human person who taught that time doesn't always seem to come afterward, even though we know it does."

"Are you talking about relativity?" asked Makr Avehl. "Really?"

"That's what he called it," said Wolf Dog, melting through a wall. "That's not what we call it. We call it messing about with things that ought to be left alone. Though of course so long as people just talk about it, no harm is done. It's when people start actually messing about with it that things start to go wrong."

"Then Gojam was right," said *Marianne*.

Makr Avehl stared at her in perplexity. It was Aghrehond who snapped his fingers in sudden memory. "He said something about Madame taking momegs and—what? Not sending them back at all?"

"To quote him exactly," said *Marianne*, Gojam said, 'She has a nasty habit of summoning up momegs on the spur of the moment, without any concern for the inconvenience it may cause, and then splatting them back again whenever it suits her.

If she returns them at all, which I have reason to doubt in some cases.' ''

Makr Avehl ran his fingers through his hair, then smoothed it, then rolled it again. "She's using them up. Burning them up, as we would burn gasoline. Through some—some mechanism, some spell, something. We need to find how she does it. If the mechanism can be destroyed—assuming she can't build another one—that will do. If the source can be eliminated, that will do."

"If Madame can be done away with," said Marianne, "that will do as well."

The others in the group looked at one another uncomfortably.

"No?" she asked, surprised.

"Not except as a last resort," Ellat said. "People like Madame—often trade off vital parts of themselves in return for power. That, too, is a shamanistic tendency. Black shaman, I should say. Those vital parts are often—well, potentiated, I suppose one might say, when the person dies."

"You're talking ghosts, here?" Marianne challenged.

"Something like that."

"So? What harm can a ghost do?"

"I'm talking real ghosts, not comic-book creatures," Ellat said patiently. "Concatenations of evil intention. Which, after sufficient aggregation, become what we would call demons. As to what harm, a very great deal. To you. To Makr Avehl. To nameless third parties we don't even know of."

"Take her word for it," said Therat, who had listened silently to the entire conversation with the momegs and who now spoke for the first time. "It would be better to render Madame helpless than to kill her. Truly. If you can figure out a way to do that, you will have done all that needs doing."

"And how do we do that?"

"We go to Lubovosk," said Makr Avehl. "We go to Lubovosk and talk to the same people Madame talked to when she learned all this. We start with the black shamans."

# CHAPTER 20

THREE BODIES AND four people went. Two Mariannes, one
Makr Avehl, one Aghrehond. Makr Avehl's beard and hair
were dyed white, he led the packhorse and walked with a cane.
Marianne wore the typical peasant dress of the region; her hair
was braided; her face was dirty. Dressed in leather trousers and
a full-sleeved shirt under a filthy sheepskin jacket, Aghrehond
drove a small flock of sheep with the help of a couple of the
momegs who showed up from time to time to nip at a lagging
heel or bark at a straying woolface. They climbed over a
mountain by a secret trail maintained by the Alphenlicht
border guards; they appeared in Lubovosk some miles inside
the border with all the requisite papers tucked in one pocket or
another.

Before they left, certain processes had been set in motion in
Alphenlicht, behind them. Functionaries at the Residence
started the day by announcing that the Prime Minister would
shortly be married, that even now his intended bride, an
American girl of impeccable Kavi descent, was visiting the
family. All attention was drawn south, to the Prime Minister's
Residence in Alphenlicht. Such had been Makr Avehl's
intention.

When advised of this ruse, Marianne was furious. "I never said I'd marry you."

"Since I didn't propose to you, that doesn't surprise me."

"You can't marry *her* unless I consent to it. It's my body, damn it."

Makr Avehl considered this for a long time, looking her up and down, walking around her as though she had been a filly for auction. "I think I could, don't you know. We'd simply divide up the time. Monday, Wednesdays, Fridays, and alternate Sundays would be yours. The other time would be ours. That would work out well, wouldn't it? You'd have lots of time to yourself. *Marianne* and I would have time to ourselves. You could learn to sleep through our times, just as Marianne did during yours."

"I'm going back to Colorado."

"That would make what I propose very difficult."

"You're impossible."

"Not impossible, no. Merely very unlikely. Face it, Marianne. We are all unlikely. You, me, Ellat, Aghrehond. The world is unlikely. But not impossible."

She had stormed at him then and did so now, clomping along the trail in her felt boots, unable to set aside her anger even for the moment.

Aghrehond caught her by the hand. "Oh, beauteous lady, most glorious master, please. For the sake of my poor, outraged heart. Here are we all, in the very belly of the beast, here on the slippery slopes of Lubovosk, here in the necromantic north, in the wicked woods, in the very gut of this dreadful country, and you argue over such trifles as who shall love whom. Truly, it may be none of us will love again, and then you will be sorry to have wasted your time in this fashion." Aghrehond sounded much aggrieved, taking out his temper on the sheep as he boomed at them to move in the direction he wished and no other. He had a tired lamb draped around his neck, which somewhat mitigated his attempts at fierceness.

Marianne subsided, though only a little. "What are we going to do when we get there? And where is there, come to that?"

Makr Avehl answered her. "We're going to the place Tabiti lives. Not a palace or residence, I've been told, but something more like a villa or chateau, outside the capital city—or what passes for one in Lubovosk. Somewhere nearby, there should be an encampment where we'll find the shamans. My spies tell me that she consults them or uses them almost daily, so they'll have to be close by. On the other hand, she wouldn't want their presence obvious to visitors, so I think they will not actually be part of her establishment.''

The sun marked their progress, from morning until noon, into the late afternoon. Along about dusk they heard the city before they saw it, a dull hum, like a hive of dispirited bees. From the crest of a hill they stared down at it, squatting like a toad in a desolate valley, surrounded by an ancient and anciently ruined wall. Here and there around the perimeter of the city were gun emplacements, and fully half the persons moving about on the streets seemed to be in uniform.

"Madame's friends," growled Makr Avehl. "Invited in to help her keep order."

"I should think she would keep order by—by her own methods," *Marianne* remarked.

"It would take too much of her time. Easier to do it by brute force and a little official terrorism, I should think. No, Madame's ambition extends far beyond this pathetic excuse for a country, believe me."

"Where's her place?"

"I see half a dozen largish houses on the surrounding hills. I think that one must be it." He pointed to the left, where a fully walled villa crowned a forested hill. "It makes some pretense at looking civilized."

"And what do we do?"

"We look around. We start by driving the sheep down that road past the place, into the woods, looking around in the woods, seeing what we see, and then pitching a tent."

"Do we have a tent?"

Aghrehond burbled, "Oh, indeed, lovely lady, we have a tent. Would we come into this despicable wilderness without some amenities for so admirable a person? What of your privacy? Your dignity? Would we come without a tent?"

"Probably," said Marianne. "Where is it?"

"On the packhorse," said Makr Avehl.

"I hope there's something for supper there as well."

"That was the idea, yes."

They passed under the walls of the chateau, studiously ignoring the impersonal insults shouted down at them by lounging guards, and went toward the forest on a narrow track.

"Smoke coming from up ahead," said Makr Avehl softly. "Could be anything, including what we're looking for." They went on, Wolf Dog and Dingo trotting behind, an ill-assorted pair of shepherds. "The shamans have a style about them. They go in for feathers and hair quite a bit. Beads, too. Also they try not to bathe very often. Not more than once every two or three years, I'd say. We may smell the camp before we see it. Or we may hear it. Shamans go in for drums, too. . . ."

Under the eaves of the forest, monstrous firs shut out the light to leave a gray-green gloom beneath their branches. From beyond a brush-covered rise, they could hear the sounds of people moving about, a muffled shout, the crack of an axe—and a drum. Makr Avehl disappeared into the brush, returning after a time brushing twigs and leaves from his jacket.

"Here, I should think," he said, nodding significantly toward the noise. While Marianne sat on a fallen log, watching them, the two men set up a camp, two small tents, a cookfire with a kettle suspended above it, and a line of ropes strung around several trees to make a pen for the sheep. When all was settled, Aghrehond and Makr Avehl began a loud and, so far as Marianne could see, pointless argument, with much shouting.

The drum which had been tum-te-tumming away behind the brush fell silent. So did the voices.

"You've forgotten it, dunderhead," growled Makr Avehl in an old man's voice. "Forgotten it completely. How can I fry sausages without my pan?"

"It was there," grumbled Aghrehond loudly and angrily. "I put it there myself."

"Greetings," said a strange voice from under the trees. "Is something wrong?"

He was tall and very dark, with feathers and beads woven into his hair. In his hand he held a staff decorated with more feathers and bones and long hanks of hair attached to chunks of skin which looked suspiciously scalplike. His mouth was bent into an obviously unaccustomed smile that displayed a few discolored teeth and did not succeed in making him look less threatening.

It was almost as though he had been expecting them, thought *Marianne*.

"This dunderhead lost my frying pan," snarled Makr Avehl.

"It's right here," said Aghrehond, triumphantly, waving it. "I told you I put it in."

"My name is Chevooskak," the dark man said with a toothy grin. The remaining teeth, though yellow, were very sharp. "Who are you?"

"Shepherds," mumbled Makr Avehl. "Trying to get these fool sheep home. Name's Dommle. He's my son. Hondi Dommle. She's his wife, Dummy Dommle. She's mute. Can't talk, thanks be. There's too much talk, anyway, in my opinion."

"Ah," murmured Chevooskak, showing his teeth once more. "Would you be interested in selling a sheep? Our camp needs meat. You could join us, if you liked. Just through the brush there. It's closer to the water than you are here."

Makr Avehl and Aghrehond discussed this while Marianne attempted to look bored and slightly half-witted. At length, Makr Avehl agreed both to sell one sheep and to move nearer to the larger camp where, on arrival, they found a dozen hide yurts arranged around a sizeable clearing with a sturdy pole coral at one side.

"You can put the sheep in there," Chevooskak said. "We won't be using it for a day or two. The horses are all out on pasture."

The language was almost the same as that spoken in Alphenlicht, though the accent was harsher. Marianne understood much of what he said, and every word made her cringe, though she could not say why.

"It's obvious why," said *Marianne*, silently. "Because he's lying to you. He intends to kill at least two of you and take the sheep."

"Which two?" she asked, then flushed. It was obvious which two. "How do you know that?"

"I just know. Ask Makr Avehl if I'm not right."

When she whispered her suspicions to Makr Avehl, he merely

nodded. "We figured on it, Marianne. Just go on as you are. Remember, you can't talk."

She was not tempted to talk aloud. Even one or two words in her unmistakeably American accent would have given them away. "What are we going to do?" she whispered.

"Wait until dark. Then do a little worm turning if the momegs will help."

"I can't see that we have any choice," said the Wolf Dog, leering at a recalcitrant sheep. "Not ethically."

Dingo merely whined and thrust her head into Marianne's lap, tongue licking delicately between Marianne's fingers.

"Why don't you ever talk?" Marianne murmured. "So silent, Dingo Dog."

"She's telepathic," said the Wolf Dog, returning the recalcitrant sheep to the corral, from which she promptly tried to escape once more. "These sheep have no brains."

"Shh," muttered Makr Avehl to the momegs. "You're going to make them suspicious with all this chatter."

Chevooskak stood at the side of the pole corral, commenting upon the edibility of various of the animals. Aghrehond argued with him vehemently. Sheep after sheep was proposed, argued over, and discarded in favor of another. When the entire flock had been considered, agreement was reached, and the stubborn wool-head who had evaded Wolf Dog was led away to the slaughter.

"Serves her right," muttered the dog.

"Quiet," urged Makr Avehl. "Sheep-dogs do not discuss their charges with the shepherd."

Fires were built. Within the hour, roasting meat smells began to drift across the clearing. Marianne found herself salivating profusely, and the dried sheet of bread which Aghrehond offered her did little to alleviate her hunger. She raised her head, sniffing, as Chevooskak brought them a fat, dripping leg, redolent of garlic and herbs.

"Welcome," he breathed at them with his toothy smile. "Welcome to our home. Eat. Enjoy."

Makr Avehl bowed, Aghrehond bowed, both cut bite-sized chunks from the meat and pretended to eat while surreptitiously tossing the chunks into the fire. Aghrehond offered a dripping slice to Marianne, gesturing pointedly at the burning fat. She took it hungrily, but managed to follow their example. Between pretend mouthfuls of the savory smelling meat, she took real bites of the dry bread along with sips of sour yoghurt.

"I think we're due to get very sleepy along about now," muttered Makr Avehl. "Tent time." He yawned ostentatiously and crept into one tent. After a moment, Aghrehond followed his example by crawling into the other one. "Get in here, wife," he bellowed. "Don't sit there dreaming by the fire."

Marianne, who had forgotten her role as Hondi Dommle's wife, started in surprise, then recovered herself and crawled into the tent where Aghrehond promptly thrust her into a corner and sat down beside the entrance, a wicked-looking knife in his hand.

"Can you call them?" he asked. "All five of them."

"That would be unnecessary," Black Dog mumbled from the pile of blankets. "We are here."

"You understand what to do?"

"A little menacing. Perhaps a bit of human chewing and tearing. A touch of mild laceration. We've done it before."

They had no opportunity to do it again for a long time. It was almost midnight before Chevooskak lurked across the clearing, a shadow among darker shadows. He paused for endless moments outside the tent, listening. Aghrehond breathed slowly, rhythmically, loudly. At last the shaman went down on all fours and crept within.

Marianne restrained herself with difficulty. The man's eyes glowed, like a cat's eyes, reflecting light.

They glowed only for a moment. Then there was a rush of bodies, a thrashing, then silence.

"Light the lantern," said Makr Avehl.

Marianne complied, feeling for the matches in the darkness. In the dim light she saw Chevooskak lying prone, one of the momegs grasping each extremity, the wolf at his throat. Aghrehond sat on the shaman's back, testing with his thumb the knife the shaman had carried.

"A simple thing," Makr Avehl said conversationally, entering the tent through a slit in the back and crouching next to Marianne. "A simple thing, Chevooskak. A request for information. These are momentary gods at your throat, at your limbs. They will not hesitate to tear you apart. You cannot control them by guile or lore, for they were not summoned by you. You see, I know some few things about this matter.''

''What do you want?'' the shaman gargled, staring sideways into the red glare of the Foo Dog's eyes. *Marianne* did not think he was as frightened as he pretended to be.

''How does Madame control the momentary gods? What device does she use? What words or incantation? How does she do it? Tell me.''

The shaman shook his head. ''She would kill me.''

''Come now. It was you who taught her in the first place.''

''Not me. No. My father taught her.''

''Well, are you not privy to your father's secrets?''

''He did not tell me everything.''

''He told you of this, though, didn't he?''

The man started to shake his head, but the dog at his throat growled softly, so he changed his mind and whispered instead. ''He said—he said he gave her the time bender.''

''What is it, this time bender?''

''I don't know. I never saw it. She has it.''

''How big a thing, then? Small, or large?''

''I don't know. Truly. I don't know!''

''Come, come.'' The momegs growled, closing their teeth upon the shaman's arms and legs. The Wolf leaned forward to get a better grip on the man's throat.

''Where did your father get it?'' whispered *Marianne*. ''Did he tell you that?'' Something was not right about this, but she couldn't tell what it was. The man's reluctance seemed real, and yet it did not. He was too easily persuaded.

''It fell. Out of the sky.''

''Let him up,'' said *Marianne*. ''I believe he will talk with us.'' And that fact disturbed her. He would talk with them. He would tell them the truth. She knew it. Why did it upset her?

Makr Avehl tied the man's hands behind him, and Aghrehond saw that two of the momegs were at either side of him before he was allowed to sit up against the canvas, glaring at them in the light of the lantern. ''Who are you?'' he hissed.

"Who?" This at least seemed an honest question. He really didn't know.

"Never mind," said *Marianne*. "You don't really want to know. Now, tell us what your father told you."

The man's eyes glazed. He mumbled a moment, "Fell from the sky, he said. Dreaming, all night, under the stars . . . stars like a great river, running away across the sky, and near morning a red star, burning, like a forge, hot over his head, east to west, falling. He went where it fell . . . all the trees bent down around it. A great hole, hot. And when it cooled, this thing was in it. So he picked it up and put it in his ghost bag and went away from there."

"So, then, we know how large it is," *Marianne* murmured. "Small enough to be carried away in his ghost bag. How big was his bag, Chevooskak? You saw it many times, how big was it?"

"So," he motioned with his hands, a small square, perhaps a foot on a side.

"With many things in it, no? Bones, perhaps?"

He nodded, unwillingly. "Many things."

"What did your father do with this time bender?"

"He could make time stop. He could make people stop moving. He could make animals stop moving. He was very powerful. Very great. Until she came."

"She," crooned *Marianne*. "Did he love her, Chevooskak?" Perhaps this was what bothered her.

The man glared, spat, honestly angry. "Like a dog after a bitch. Everything he knew, he told her. Everything he had, he gave her."

"Instead of to you, his son?"

The shaman growled, deep in his throat. "When she had it all, she killed him."

*Marianne* looked at Makr Avehl and shrugged. This last was real, very real. Chevooskak felt that. The other? She was not comfortable with what little they had learned, but she knew of no way to get at the source of her discomfort. Makr Avehl leaned forward to press his hands on the shaman's neck. The shaman fell forward, unconscious, and the momegs stepped fastidiously away from him.

"He smells terrible," said the Blue Dragon Dog." "I don't think he ever bathes."

"I would have hated to bite him," admitted Wolf Dog, "though honor would have constrained me to do so."

"It wasn't necessary," commented Makr Avehl. "*Marianne* seems to have found out what we needed to know. Let's dose him with that potion Ellat gave me, Hondi, then haul him back to his yurt. The potion should guarantee he remembers none of this." He turned to Marianne with a puzzled look, a look he retained when he returned to the tent. "Don't you think that was too easy?" he murmured.

"Perhaps not," Aghrehond argued, without real conviction. "He is not the man his father was. That is clear. Perhaps the power which would have passed from father to son passed instead to her—Madame?"

"Possible," Makr Avehl acknowledged, "but I still think it was much too easy." The expression of concern stayed on his face and was still there early in the morning, before most of the camp was astir, when they left with their flock. Chevooskak came out of his yurt to stare bleary-eyed after them, a look of confusion on his face.

"Too easy," said Makr Avehl again.

"I wish you wouldn't keep saying that," said Marianne. "It doesn't seem easy to me. You may know more or less what you're looking for, but you still have no idea where she keeps it or what it really looks like."

"We know a few things about it," said Makr Avehl. "She uses it to move people into her false worlds. She used it on *Marianne*—my Marianne—at the top of a flight of stairs in Marianne's own house. She had it with her. Was she carrying anything at that time?"

*Marianne* answered. "Nothing but a clipboard with a piece of paper on it. Nothing in her hands."

"And what was she wearing?"

"A cap, like a uniform cap, and dark shirt and trousers, I think. Yes. I'm sure. I thought she was a delivery person until she raised her head."

"Shirt and trousers. Nothing voluminous. Something, then,

that would fit in a pocket or, more likely, on a chain around the neck.''

"She never wears low-cut clothes," *Marianne* said. "I have been trying to remember every time I've seen her. She always wore a high-necked dress or shirt.''

"So, we assume when she leaves her home, she wears the thing around her neck. When she's at home, however, she could put it almost anywhere.''

"So," Aghrehond continued, "we have a better chance if we get her to come out than if we go in after her.''

Marianne snorted. "How do you expect to do that?''

"Very simple," said Makr Avehl. "We invite her to the wedding.''

# CHAPTER 21

MARIANNE WAS FURIOUS. "I know why he's doing it. I know it's a good plan. I know Madame will probably come like a shot, if just to have a chance at me! But this kind of haste—well, it's unseemly, that's what it is. People will think I'm pregnant."

Ellat said reasonably, "Well, what's that matter in this day and age? What's that matter in any day and age, come to that? Even here in Alphenlicht, it's not that unusual."

"Papa will split a gusset," Marianne snarled, quoting Cloud-haired Mama, who always asserted that Papa would split a gusset. Marianne herself had no very clear idea of what a gusset might be. "He'll name a new executor. He'll . . . Besides, I don't want to get married."

"My brother won't be marrying you, dear."

"You tell me how he's going to marry *her* without marrying *me*. We just happen to be sharing a body. There are certain— intimacies that go with marriage you know." She stopped, flushing. When it came right down to it, she could not be repelled by the idea of those intimacies, though she tried. "It's like rape," she told herself vehemently, not believing a word of it. Her body—*their* body—refused to consider it rape.

"My dear, be calm. Please. Be calm. Makr Avehl will do nothing to offend your sensibilities, you have my word. Take a nap. You look tired."

"I do nothing these days but take naps. I slept half of yesterday. Don't try to put me off, Ellat. It's international news. Papa will hear of it."

"Leave that to the Prime Minister, my dear. He will handle everything."

Marianne subsided, wondering as she did so where the other *Marianne* had taken herself. Though her presence could still be felt, she had not recently interrupted or taken over. She yawned. It was true that she seemed to do nothing but sleep, lately. And she was becoming forgetful. This morning when she woke from a quick nap, she was not wearing the same blouse she remembered having on when she lay down. This morning, she remembered putting her slippers on one side of the bed and woke to find them on the other. Why did Marianne have this feeling that something was going on, that *Marianne* and Makr Avehl were plotting something, when they could not possibly plot anything without her knowing. Was there some way that *Marianne* could remain active while Marianne was asleep? "Lying low, are you?" she snarled at the mirror. "If I could get my hands on you."

All Alphenlicht had been delighted to learn that the wedding would take place only a few weeks hence. A couturier had been summoned from Paris to create a wedding gown, and the tiny state newspaper had run pictures of previous gowns created by this master. The menu for the nuptial banquet was published, occasioning much comment, particularly on the matter of wines. The Residence servants brought in their cousins and sisters and started an orgy of cleaning out and refurbishing. Various members of the Kavi were said to be rehearsing the rituals that would be used. Plate and porcelain were unpacked and polished. It would be a small wedding. Only three hundred guests were invited, virtually all of them from Alphenlicht.

Marianne did not recall being interviewed, but various international publications ran stories about her, quoting her views on the Alphenlicht-Lubovosk controversy, on feminism, on agricultural management. One writer commented on the soundness of her opinions concerning sheep. Her image smiled brightly from the pages of *Time* and *Newsweek,* Makr Avehl's striking darkness looming protectively in the background.

Cloud-haired Mama called. Papa called. Somehow neither of them was as upset as Marianne had supposed they might be. Somehow she was unable to tell either of them that she was being kidnapped, shanghaied, invaded by an alternate self and married off without her consent. Even during her phone conversations with them, she yawned, sleepily, wondering what was going on.

A week in advance of the ceremony, there was to be a small "family" dinner, to which certain aunts and uncles and cousins were invited, along with some of the Kavi and Marianne's parents. A special messenger was sent to deliver an invitation for Tabiti Delubovoska to attend this event.

"I worded it very carefully," said Ellat. "Along the lines of 'let bygones by bygones, join us in celebration, all one heritage after all.' I have no idea if she'll believe any of it, or even if she thinks I believe it, but it should do the job."

"I wouldn't believe it," said Marianne, flatly. "I don't think she will either. She won't think it's natural."

"It all seems very natural," objected Makr Avehl. "Our getting married."

"To you, perhaps," Marianne jeered. "It feels anything but natural to me. Besides, that's not what I meant. I meant after everything we've been through with her, she won't think the invitation is natural. As to this putative wedding, I still haven't agreed to go through with it!"

"Well, perhaps it won't be necessary to go through with it."

"And what do you mean by that?" Her heart had stopped, and she was trying to cope with an emotional flood. Surely she didn't want to marry the man! Then why this terror at the thought she might not?

"We believe Madame will make her move at the family dinner," said Ellat. "And, if she does, and if we are successful, then one of the major reasons for the wedding will have vanished. . . ."

"The family dinner! Mama and Papa will be here. She might do something to them!"

"No, they won't be here. They'll be delayed, in Paris. I've arranged for that. They'll have to charter a plane to get here, and I've arranged for that, too. They won't get here until after—well, after."

"So—it's just me and you, and Ellat, and Aghrehond."

"And a few aunts and uncles, and Therat, and Cyram, and Nalavi. A dozen or two people. Nothing threatening at all."

Marianne wasn't at all sure of that. She could not get it out of her head that something was going on that she didn't know about.

"You know, this dress looks familiar to me, and yet I know I've never had one like it." Marianne looked at herself in the mirror, glittering and swaying in her silver sequined sheath. "It was kind of you to order it for me, Ellat."

"Well, that silly man was making such a fuss over one wedding dress, I decided he needed something to occupy his mind. I've had him do half a dozen things for me, as well. I even talked Therat into having a few gowns made. She's such a dear woman—though Makr Avehl claims to find her scary, she's really very sensible—but she's never paid any attention to clothes at all. Before you came along, my dear, I often hoped that she and Makr Avehl would get to know one another better." Ellat smiled sweetly at her, and Marianne felt something clutch her stomach at the thought of Makr Avehl and Therat.

"Still, the gown does look familiar," she faltered, needing to say something.

"Well, you know, the other *Marianne* may have had one like it." Did have, Ellat told herself. Definitely did have. Fought Madame off in it, she did, for a whole evening. She pressed a hand flat on her own stomach, quieting the slightly sick feeling of apprehension that kept coming and going, remembering a recent conversation with Makr Avehl.

*"My dear, it is so risky my heart stops, thinking of it!"*

*"Of course it's risky, Ellat. Life is risky. However, you yourself said we had to confront her. So, we're going to confront her."*

*"She'll twist. She'll fight. She'll bite you like a serpent, brother."*

*"She will that. She'll come in all smiles, but she'll plan to
leave with me dead and Marianne in her pocket."*

*"You've been to the Cave?"*

*"You know I have, dear Ellat. The Cave says fishes. Whole
walls full of fishes. Therat thinks she has it figured out."*

*"And yet she's letting you go ahead?"*

*He shook his head at her, sadly. "Let, Ellat? Let? It has to be
done, and that's all there is to it."*

Now she took Marianne's hand to descend the curving main
stair of the Residence, smiling bravely and wondering if she
were going to be able to eat anything at all.

The guests arrived. There was much sparkle and laughter,
many congratulations for Makr Avehl, many good wishes for
Marianne. Tabiti arrived in a long, black limousine, escorted by
a much bemedaled officer of uncertain rank. She twinkled and
glittered, congratulating Makr Avehl, exclaiming over
Marianne's dress, falling fulsomely upon Ellat's neck, her eyes
and mouth in ceaseless motion.

The guests drank champagne, ate hors d'ouevres, chatted.
Dinner was announced. The guests were seated. Tabiti was
down the table from Makr Avehl and Marianne, separated from
Ellat by only one guest. Marianne could not take her eyes from
Madame's dramatically high-necked gown. At the throat was a
spider done in jet-black beads, and the web extended across the
bosom of the dress and down the long sleeves. Butterflies in
bright sequins lay upon this web, seeming to struggle as
Madame moved and laughed and turned to throw long, significant glances up the table.

"What is she going to do?" Marianne demanded.

"Shhh, my love," said Makr Avehl. "Smile. Finish your
consommé."

A whole fish on a vast silver tray was carried to the buffet to
be carved and served with many flourishes while the footmen
poured wine.

The guests tasted, approved, ate hungrily.

"What kind of fish is this?" Marianne asked Makr Avehl. "I
don't think I've seen the kind before."

He shook his head at her. "Something the cook found," he

said rather loudly. "She's a marvel, that woman. I ought to give her a raise."

For all his admiration, he didn't seem to be eating much of it. Then the fish was gone. The plates and one set of wine glasses were cleared away. . . .

And the world slowed down.

Voices fell lower and lower, like a record played a slow speed, lower until they stopped.

Faces moved less and less until they did not move at all.

Hands with glasses in them remained halfway to lips, which remained half parted.

"You should have paid more attention to where your cook got her fish, Prime Minister," said Madame, the words ringing down the long table like a struck anvil, hard and metallic. "A vengeance fish, that one, from a certain world of mine, a world perhaps you remember? I named that fish with the names of everyone at this table. Cold, that fish, and now cold all of those here. Unmoving, that fish, and now unmoving all those here. Except myself and my escort, of course. And now, if you and Marianne don't mind coming with me?" She stood, smiling. Marianne found herself getting up and walking, though she was not conscious of any volition to do so. She was beside Makr Avehl. They were walking out of the Residence, getting into Madame's car. "At the border," Madame instructed, "you will tell your people you are going to Lubovosk with me for a nightcap. It's only fifteen miles. Tell them you'll be back by midnight. And you will be back. You and your little love, here. Both of you will be back."

"He said it was too easy," thought Marianne. "We weren't waiting for her. She was waiting for us." Then she couldn't think any more for it took too much effort.

The car drove away. Marianne wondered, vaguely, what the servants at the Residence would think when they came to clear for the next course and found all the guests sitting there, frozen. Perhaps the servants wouldn't come in at all. Perhaps Madame had named a fish for them, as well.

"Do you know, dear girl, I have had dreams about you," said Madame in the car as it sped through the darkness toward the high, guarded border. "I dreamed once that your dear brother, my nephew, Haurvatat—named for your father by my dear dead sister who was his first wife—I dreamed that Harvey had not had his unfortunate accident and that he and I were able to entertain you as we had once planned. I dreamed once that your dear parents had succumbed to some misfortune and died. Then I woke, and it was all a dream. Was it a dream, little Marianne?"

Marianne felt a compulsion to answer, to tell the entire story of what had happened to Harvey and her own part in it. Her lips opened, her tongue vibrated . . .

And *Marianne* said calmly, "It must have been a dream. Poor Harvey had an accident."

"How did I do that?" Marianne asked from deep within herself. "How?"

"She forgot to name the fish for me," said *Marianne*, silently. "She named it for only one of us, and that one was you."

Madame looked dissatisfied, as though the answer she had received was not the one she had expected. "Only a dream, Marianne? Are you quite sure?"

"Harvey had an accident," said *Marianne* in a child's voice. "It was very sad. Papa cried."

"That's too bad," said Madame, petulantly. "When I dream, I remember it otherwise."

The car stopped at the border. In an emotionless voice, Makr Avehl gave the message he had been directed to give. The car sped on.

"In my dream," Madame went on, "Harvey inherited a great deal of wealth. I let him enjoy parts of it, though most came to me. With it, I was able to subvert some of the Prime Minister's key supporters. With it, I planned to gain control of the Cave of Light."

"Yes," said *Marianne* in an uninflected voice, like a sigh. "That is what you planned to do."

"We had only to remove you, little Marianne, when we had made what use of you we could. It was all planned, how we would do it. In my dream. There would be dogs, and a horse, and an accident. In my dream. But it was Harvey who had the accident.''

"Papa cried," said *Marianne*, again.

Madame was sulkily silent for some miles. When she spoke again, the car was on the high ridge above the city.

"We are going to my villa. Not that it's really necessary to do so. I could have concluded my business with you anywhere, but I wanted to do it there. So I could remember it, later. . . .

"I have a room there, in my villa, in the tower at the back of the garden. There are windows all around it. I take my tower to all my worlds, did you know that? Wherever I go, there is a tower there. On the embassy. On the palace. On the library. In the center of town. Somewhere, there is always a tower. . . .

"Always a tower," agreed *Marianne*.

"That's where I'm taking you and your lover. When you are my servants, you and the Prime Minister, I will sit in my high, lovely tower and remember how it came about. Won't that be amusing?"

Again Marianne felt a terrible compulsion to tell the truth, to say, "No, it will be horrible."

But *Marianne* answered for her in a low, emotionless voice, "Amusing."

Madame pouted. She had wanted more sport than this. In the seat across from her, Makr Avehl sat motionless, his eyes fixed before him as though he saw something there from which he could not move his gaze. Silence as the car rushed on. The city fled away to their right. They began to climb the hill on which the villa stood. Before them, gates swung open onto a dark courtyard. As they went through the gates, the headlights disclosed several figures outside the wall, tall, with feathers in their hair and high, scalp-decked staffs.

"Dear Chevooskak," murmured Madame. "Come to see if you've arrived safely."

"It was too easy," thought Marianne.

"Shhh," said *Marianne*. "We thought so, too."

"And here we are." Madame alighted from the car, summoning men who came to take each of Makr Avehl's arms, each of Marianne's. "I thought you might like a tour of the villa.

You've never been here, Makr Avehl.'' She laughed, a tiny frozen glitter of sound. "You know, in my dream, I once thought we would be married, you and I. Oh, I know I'm somewhat older than you, but still—it would have reunified our countries. You would have enjoyed it Makr Avehl.''

"I would rather have died,'' said Makr Avehl, like an automaton.

"That, too, can be arranged,'' said Madame.

They went into the villa, through a wide hall and into a long gallery. "I call this my gallery of worlds,'' Madame said as she turned on the lights. "It will amuse you both. See, here is a favorite world of mine.''

Marianne stared at the picture, a long avenue ending at the Gates of Darius. There was scaffolding against the Gates, and dwarfs huddled upon it, pecking at the stones with tiny hammers. Far down the Avenue shone the pale stones of the embassy, and it seemed to Marianne that she might see herself drifting aimlessly down that Avenue toward that building. . . .

"Or this one,'' said Madame. "Not one of mine, originally, but I rather like it.''

A peculiar city under a lowering sky, with tattered posters covering almost every wall. Marianne shuddered, without knowing she had done so. Somewhere in that city, something violent and horrible was abroad, hunting. She knew it.

"Or this,'' said Madame.

A stretch of lawn before the tall, slender pillars of the palace. Twin fountain basins at either side. And at the back of the building, a tower, at one of the windows of which a curtain twitched as though someone were watching.

"But this is one I want you to pay particular attention to, Prime Minister. Marianne. Look.''

The world was covered with water. In one place, the remains of a mud tower protruded above the surface, crumbling even as they watched. A long avenue of stakes had been driven into the shallow water, and chained to these were a variety of creatures, one of which had multiple eyes and legs and arms and an expression of patient terror.

"Gojam,'' said *Marianne*. "She caught him.''

"The silly creatures who live there called in the tide,''

yawned Madame. "Now I use it to keep things in. Things—and people." She sighed. "Enough. It's time we went up to my tower, Marianne, to my lovely room, Makr Avehl. The little elevator is just over here. You may release my guests now, gentlemen. They will be quite safe with me. . . ."

The guards went away. They were in a tiny box which purred its way upward, quite alone except for Madame. She let them out into a high room surrounded by arched windows. Curtains closed these arches against the dark sky, but Madame made a slow circuit of the room, opening them to let the stars look in.

"We need only a little light to do what we will do. Starlight is enough, don't you think?"

They did not answer.

She fished in the neck of her gown and drew out a little sack. From the sack she took something, a small something, the size of a walnut, and set it upon a table at the center of the room.

It shone, a twisting of light. It glimmered with lines and points of shining white. As their eyes fastened upon it, it grew. Where there had been only a few points of light, there were now many. Where there had been only two or three spiraling lines, now there were hundreds. . . .

"The time bender," gloated Madame. "What people do you suppose created it, Prime Minister? What starship do you suppose it was on? What unimaginable accident caused it to crash on our world? And what luck, for me, that old Chevooskak Anuk found it. And what luck, for me, that he found me irresistible." She laughed, a quiver of sound so cold that even in her ice-bound lethargy, Marianne shivered.

"You shouldn't have sought out his son, Prime Minister. I listen in on all Chevooskak's thoughts, all his conversations. He does what I tell him. When he told you about the time bender, I heard it all. He did only what I told him to do, said only what I told him to say. Even his fury at me, I told him to let you see that. It's true enough. He hates me, but he obeys me. Old Chevooskak Anuk might have been able to protect himself against me—though he never would have—but his son, no."

She began to dance around the twist of light, a slow, bending waltz, humming to herself as she did so. "What shall we do with it tonight? Eh? I had thought to send you and Makr Avehl away for a time, to that wet world you traveled before. You would not escape from it now. I would leave you there, chained to a stake, for a time. Only a hundred years or so. And then bring you back when only an hour had passed. Would you love one another then, I wonder? After a hundred years up to your hips in water, with only the mud creatures to talk to? You are their law giver, Prime Minister. I have no doubt they would feed you the very best of their scum. . . .

"Or shall we simply set the chains upon you both now and forget the amusement?" She whirled, her skirts swirling around her, her arms raised, a dervish of evil intent. "Yes. I think we will set the chains of servitude upon you. Bind you in time. Forever."

"Now," called *Marianne* in her mind. "Now, Dingo Dog. Now, momegs! Do it now, do it now!"

From somewhere beneath Madame's feet, a howling broke loose, a hideous caterwauling so clamorous that Madame clapped her hands to her ears, eyes slitted. "What?" she grated. "What?"

Marianne and Makr Avehl were unmoving, seeming not to hear. The sound renewed itself, even louder. There were screams and shouts of people mixed in with a kind of barking yodel, the sound of a pack on the hunt.

Madame twitched, snarled. "Do wait for me children," she instructed, pointing her long, bony fingers at each of them. "Don't run away." Then she was back in the little elevator, the door closing behind her.

As soon as they were alone, *Marianne* walked calmly to the table where the time bender stood and took it into her hand. "She didn't name me at all, did she? Just as you thought, Makr Avehl, she didn't know I was there." *Marianne* leaned forward and snapped her fingers beneath his nose, seeing him twitch into sudden life. "Come on, love. We're going away from here just as we planned. But first, there are a few things I need to do."

# CHAPTER 22

THERE WERE NO words in her mind at all. None of the tools of thinking were there, not yet. Nonetheless, she saw faces peering down at her, saw smiles on lips, heard chortling words and knew them. They were people. The words of recognition came swimming through her mind like familiar fish. Mama. Papa. Great-aunt Dagma.

She was three days old.

"Third time is the charm," said *Marianne*.

# CHAPTER 23

"THE WEDDING WAS very, very beautiful," said Cloud-haired Mama. "I was so afraid we'd miss it. When we got held up in Paris that way, I thought for sure you'd have to get married without us!"

"Even I thought it was lovely," Marianne laughed, "once you and Papa got here. Though I was afraid you'd think it was terribly sudden."

"No more sudden than the way Haurvatat married me. He met me on the third of June and by the tenth we were married. They have this way with them, the men of Alphenlicht. And he's as happy for you as I am, Mist Princess. Though how you got here and married when the last thing we knew you were in Denver, working for the feds—that's what Papa says—'the feds'. . . ."

"Well, as you said, the men of Alphenlicht have a way with them. Makr Avehl just wouldn't rest until I came here, and I'd no sooner arrived than he announced the wedding."

"I do hope he proposed properly in between."

"You know, I really can't remember. He must have, don't you think? Surely I wouldn't have consented to a wedding if he hadn't proposed?"

"Of course not, darling. Look, there's Papa beckoning to me. He has someone he wants me to meet." And Cloud-haired Mama drifted away across the room looking almost as young and lovely as Marianne herself.

"Happy?" asked Makr Avehl from behind her. "Would you like more champagne?"

She turned and kissed him, feeling her whole body come alive as she pressed against him, catching her breath in a shaky laugh as she said, "Very happy. But I haven't had any champagne at all, yet. You've been hogging it all for yourself."

"Lovely wedding," murmured Ellat, offering her a glass and a curious look, both at once. "I was thinking during the ceremony how little you've changed, Marianne. When you first arrived here in Alphenlicht, you were a bit of a stranger, but now you're so much the girl I knew—before."

"Oh, I finally got myself together," laughed Marianne, looking up at Makr Avehl with a twinkle. "Or we did. I think personalities tend to integrate as we get a little older, don't you, Ellat? Most of us are rather schizy when we're young."

"There's certainly nothing the matter with your integration," Ellat admitted with a continuing searching look into Marianne's face. There was a lot of courage there, and determination. A lot of intelligence, too, as well as an almost violent alacrity, given to sudden decisions. Ellat was looking for a kind of untried girlishness that she thought she remembered seeing recently, but it wasn't there. She tipped her glass in salute and smiled again as she moved away. It had been a beautiful wedding.

"Isn't it time we were running off somewhere?" Marianne whispered to Makr Avehl. "Isn't it time you were taking me to bed, love?"

"Forward wench." He grinned at her, eating her with his eyes. "Just a few more minutes and we'll escape. I hadn't told you, but we're going up to the hunting lodge for a proper honeymoon. We can leave in just a bit, but I think there are just one or two guests who may put in an appearance. . . ."

There was a momentary hush from across the room as one of the belated guests arrived—a very old woman, leaning on the arms of two attendants. Her hair was white and her expression was mildly vacant.

"Oh, look," said Marianne in a voice that anyone who did not know her very well would have thought to be sympathetic. "Isn't that Tabiti Delubovoska? One of Papa's relatives by his first marriage. I met her once when I was only a child. She's aged terribly. Heavens, she must be ninety-five if she's a day." She smiled up at Makr Avehl again, seeing his eyes riveted on the old woman.

"Over a hundred," he offered. "So I've been told. Though she looked remarkably young for her age until just—well, recently."

"Pity," said Marianne, drinking her champagne. "I don't think she'll last much longer. Well, we women can only hold time at bay for so long. It gets all of us in the end."

"Does it indeed?" asked Makr Avehl. "Does it, Marianne?"

They stood looking at one another for a long moment, each still holding a celebratory glass in hand. Makr Avehl's expression was loving, watchful, a little wary, as though something had happened of which he was only partially aware. "Does time get all of us in the end?"

"Of course," said Marianne, touching her breast where something hung on a chain beneath her high-necked dress. Across the room, a black dog with Gojam on its back poked its head through a door and winked at her.

Marianne looked up at her lover and smiled.

"Of course it does, darling," she said.

# Fantasy from Ace
# fanciful and fantastic!